MOONLIGHT AND MIDTOWN

A FAIRY TALES OF THE MAGICORUM NOVELLA 1.5

CHRISTINA BAUER

Brighton, MA 02135

www.monsterhousebooks.com

ISBN 9781945723469

❀ Created with Vellum

DEDICATION

For All Those Who Kick Ass, Take Names, And Read Books

7 p.m. Time to get dressed. In other words, time to change from "seventeen-year-old slob" into "cool Manhattan socialite." Crossing my bedroom, I open my closet door and wince. A few holiday-themed sweaters line the top shelf. Clusters of bare wooden hangers knock against one another, wind-chime style. Out of my once-awesome collection of footwear, only two lonely flip-flips now collect dust on the floor. They don't even match.

No question about it. Being a werewolf is a murder on your wardrobe.

And I have an art opening to attend tonight. Bummer.

On reflex, I turn around, ready to sift through the contents of my dresser. Then I remember I don't have a dresser anymore. Whenever I shift, I lock myself in my bedroom. My wolf smashed all the furniture in here weeks ago. In fact, she really destroyed my dresser, gnawing the wood into chips. These days, my bedroom's decorated with a single mattress and tons of claw marks on the walls. I've taken to keeping my underthings in a drawer in the bathroom.

A sad weight settles onto my shoulders. My aunties kept me

locked in a penthouse so they could hide my true magical nature from me. With the help of my bf Knox and my bff Elle, I broke free from their plans and tricks. There's no hiding the truth from me any more. I can wield all three types of magic: fairy, shifters, and witch. Even so, I'm still trapped in my apartment because who wants to spontaneously shift into a werewolf on Fifth Avenue and then end up naked on the sidewalk?

Not me.

But tonight's art opening is with other Magicorum kids like me, so shifting shouldn't be a big deal. Plus, my boyfriend Knox will be there with me, and he's a were Alpha, so he can help me control when I change forms.

All of which leads to the fact that I need something to wear tonight.

Back to the closet I go.

For a full minute, I stare at the empty hangers as if my old wardrobe will somehow magically reappear. Not happening.

Every time I shift, I shred another outfit. And lately, I've been shifting a ton. Some mornings, my wolf tears out six times before I down my bagel, and it's all because I first took my werewolf form only a month ago on my seventeenth birthday. Most weres spend a lifetime mastering their wolf. I've had four weeks.

At least I have a master plan to fix my wardrobe issue: a shopping spree in Manhattan's secret network of stores run by the fae. My best friend Elle is taking me because she's both fae and an awesome shopping partner. With any luck, Elle and I will find me some unshreddable magic outfits. That is, if I survive the trip. Fairies are crazy. Plus, most carry a major grudge against weres. About a million years ago, some weres lost their cool and tried to massacre some fae. They didn't succeed, but fairies have a long memory, and shifters are definitely on their hate list.

Speaking of weres, my inner wolf speaks to me in my mind. As always, her voice combines silky tones with a gruff edge. *"Where is our mate?"*

She's talking about Knox. I'm not totally comfortable with calling him my mate yet, even though—let's face it—that's what he is.

I reply to her in my thoughts. *"Knox is on his way. We're going to that art opening tonight, remember?"*

"How disappointing." My inner animal has a pretty good vocabulary for anyone, but especially for a wolf. I think it's because she spent her first eighteen years trapped inside a spell where she could only listen and watch me do stuff. *"I'd rather visit the forest, you know."*

My stomach twists. I'm not a total fan of tonight's plans, either.

Knox and I are about to attend a swanky art show featuring students from West Lake Prep, my future high school. It's now June; school starts in September. Tonight I'll meet my new classmates for the very first time. Plus, considering how I've been home-schooled all my life, this marks the first time I'll meet any fellow students, period.

Whoa.

Long story short, there is no way I'm showing up tonight in a Christmas sweater-dress and mismatched flip-flops. I need something else to wear.

My anxiety feeds in to my inner wolf's discomfort. Deep within my soul, she paces and growls. My wolf wants to shift, run, and be free from everything. That same urge fills me as well. Within seconds, my limbs twitch to change forms. I push down on that desire with my will, but I can only hold back for so long.

Closing my eyes, I make some quick calculations. Based on how my wolf's acting, I have an hour, tops, before she pops out of my skin. So before those sixty minutes are up, I have to get dressed, haul my cookies to the opening, and make a quick combination of hello and goodbye.

Not a moment to waste.

Time to borrow an outfit from my roommate. I pull open my bedroom door and call out into the hallway.

"Elle?"

Elle is my roomie and best friend. We're both members of the Magicorum, and each member has the power of a fairy, witch, or shifter inside us. It also counts if you have a direct relative with magic. In any case, most Magicorum have only one power—Elle's is fairy magic—but for some reason, I have all three. My abilities tore loose a month ago when I battled an army of zombie-mummies called the Denarii along with their leader, a creepster named Jules. Ever since then, my fairy and witch powers haven't shown up again, which is fine with me. I'm having enough trouble with my inner wolf.

I raise my voice a little. "Elle?"

In reply, I hear the *click-clack* of computer keyboards followed by the low rumble of arguing voices. I'd know that particular set of noises anywhere. It's the distinct soundtrack of Elle playing a videogame with a buddy.

I frown. *That can't be right.* Elle started playing Kazimir's Gate last night with Alec, our friend who happens to be the heir to the Le Charme dynasty of jewelry stores. Those two couldn't still be playing, could they?

I step down the hallway and into our living room. It's a wide space with bay windows, leather furniture, and tons of electronics. Sure enough, Elle and Alec are camped out on our big couch, wireless keyboards perched on their laps.

Unbelievable but true. Those two have been at it for more than twenty-four hours straight.

I step closer. "Hey, guys. I thought you were quitting ages ago. We're supposed to leave for the art opening, right?"

Elle waves to me from the couch. "No worries," she says. "We're almost done with the Mushuu mines."

For the thousandth time, it strikes me how my best friend looks just like Cinderella, what with her long golden-blonde hair and big blue eyes. The only difference from the Grimm Brother's version of Cinderella and my bestie is that my Elle wears modern clothes. Today, that means leggings and a white button down. The same is true for Alec, too. The guy is a dead ringer for Prince Charming, but one who's wearing jeans and a T-shirt.

By the way, the whole fairy tale look-alike thing is no coincidence. Both Elle and Alec have magic—he's a warlock—which means they're also part of the Magicorum. Members of the Magicorum are supposed to live according to a fairy tale life template. Elle's is definitely Cinderella, while Alec's is Prince Charming. In my case, my template is supposed to be Sleeping Beauty. I've got the brown hair, slim build, and blue eyes that go along with the story, too. That said, being a shifter is not part of the tale, let alone the fact that I wield all three kinds of magic. It's weird. Most days, I just try not to think about it.

Denial. It's not just a river in Egypt.

I'm still in the living room, but I'm not sure Elle or Alec has even registered my existence. Instead, my bestie is glaring daggers at Alec.

"Hold on there," says Elle. "What's wrong with you? Why didn't you take a healing potion before we went into battle?"

"I took the dumb potion." Alec squints at the screen. "Oops, maybe not."

"And now we have to fight this rabid squirrel."

"It's an undead Wyvern."

For the record, I understand the sweet perfection of sharing a cool new two-person game. Elle and I spend many hours on Skyrim. But still.

I clear my throat. "So, are you guys going or not?"

Elle keeps right on glaring at Alec. "Are you crazy? No healing potion?" Her face burns red with fury. This is a rare sight. My bestie never loses her cool. "This monster has eight thousand hit points. You've been getting your ass kicked."

"I have four hundred hit points."

"Before the ass kicking. Now you have..." Elle leans forward as she squints at the screen. "Two hit points left. My friend, you will be D-E-A-D before we even make a dent on this bad guy."

"My dear Elle, how you underestimate me." Alec grins. He's totally working his Prince Charming vibe here. But with Alec, that look mixes with a surfer-dude edge, what with his tanned skin and loose blond hair. He winks at Elle. "We can kill this. I found a sword of 'Plus A Million Hit Points Of Awesomeness.' One strike, and that thing is history."

Elle rolls her eyes. "You're such a cheater." Even so, there's no anger in her words. Elle is a total con artist. She only works her schemes for a good cause, though. That said, Elle always appreciates a clever cheat. She and Alec would make a great pair if they ever decided to date. But so far, that hasn't been in the cards. I can't get a straight story out of Elle, but it all has something to do with my bestie's evil stepfamily.

"Ahem." I move to stand right behind the couch. "I said, are you guys still going?"

It's Alec who waves at me this time. "Sure, we are." His shoulders shiver as he types furiously on his keyboard. Kazimir's Gate is best played on a keyboard instead of a controller, and Alec is tough on equipment. We've gone through three keyboards in the last month.

"How will that work, exactly?" I ask. "You've both been up all night. No offense, but you don't smell ready to go." I sniff. *Truth.*

Keeping his gaze glued to the monitor, Alec nods toward a side chair. His sport coat lies slung over the armrest. "I have some new gemstones in my pockets. When the time is right, I'll cast a spell to get us ready. Won't take a minute." Gemstones are how wizards store extra power for a casting. "After that, I'll cast a transport spell for the Belvedere Gallery."

Anxiety tightens up my back. "The Belvedere Gallery? That place is teeny-tiny. I thought the opening was at the Ritz ballroom."

"Change of venue," explains Alec. "Word leaked that there was a Magicorum event at the Ritz. Humans were already camping out on the sidewalk. You know how it is. We had to change properties."

Unfortunately, this kind of thing happens all the time. Magic is disappearing from the world, and the Magicorum are vanishing as well. Humans see us as photo opps. Ever since I found out I was a were, I've been convinced that *"she's a shifter"* is somehow written on my forehead in bright neon letters. There's no shaking the sense that someone is following me, ready to take a photo. Of all the humans who stalk Magicorum, howlers are the worst. They're the ones who stalk weres. They have their own hidden internet called the furry-web where they post pictures and videos of shifters in embarrassing situations. It's involves a lot of bare butts.

I shiver. There is no way I want my ass on the internet.

That said, having stalkers is not my biggest worry right now. The fact that I'm going to the Belvedere freaks out my wolf in a serious way. Confined spaces are not her thing. She paces inside my soul at a more furious speed.

"No small rooms," whispers my wolf. *"I beg you. Woods."*

The urge to shift strikes me again. Once more, fur ripples under my skin. Did I think I had an hour before I was forced to shift? It might be a matter of minutes.

I rub my neck in a nervous rhythm. "You know what, guys? I'm not sure this art opening is a great idea. If my wolf breaks out, she could trash the place."

Alec sniffs. "My family owns the gallery. We have specially trained guards there in case anyone's magic side gets out of control. Don't worry."

"Please," whispers my wolf. *"We must run."*

The drive to shift becomes even stronger. My bones shimmy and twist inside me. The movement doesn't hurt me, though. It's just the idea of being forced to change again that's so painful.

Sure, Alec says that I can ruin my bedroom all I want—his family owns this building, too, after all—but that still doesn't sit well with me. I don't like destroying stuff, and I really hate losing control of my own body.

Taking a half step backward, I make for the safety of my room. "I think I better stay home."

Moving in unison, Alec and Elle hit the Pause key and look over the back of the couch at me.

"I know you're worried about your wolf," says Elle.

"Wouldn't you be?" I mime someone taking a photo. "There are howlers everywhere."

Elle wags her finger. "You can't hide out in the apartment forever."

"Why not? We have high-speed internet and lots of snacks." I try to make this sound like a joke, but it comes off as a little desperate.

"Bry, this summer is your chance to get used to your wolf form."

"So tonight is what, wolf training?" I ask.

Alec nods. "Why do you think we're having this at my property with my guards?"

A weight of guilt settles into my stomach. "You shouldn't have gone through all that trouble for me. I'll be fine come September." *Total lie.*

"What are friends for?" Alec's face warms with another winning smile. "This is my gallery with my hired people. Plus, the students are cool. Everyone's either in the Magicorum or related to someone who is. Trust me, there's nothing they haven't seen. This will be a great way to start testing your wolf in public."

Elle smacks her lips. "Of course, if you're not up for it, you can always stay home." My bestie gives me a sly look. She knows all about what I call my rebel-reflex. Tell me I'm not up for something, and I simply must prove I can do it.

My mouth starts moving on its own. "Oh, I'm going all right."

An image pops into my head: my almost-empty closet. "Only, can I borrow something of yours to wear?"

Elle grins. "I thought you'd never ask."

"Meaning?"

"Take what you want. Knock yourself out."

Wow. I lift my arms with my palms forward in the universal hand signal for *stop right there.* "Full disclosure," I say. "No matter what you loan me, it will probably get destroyed."

Elle shrugs. "I love to shop. You've got a talent right now for ruining wardrobes. This is a win-win in my opinion." Elle returns her attention to the megascreen and pounds on keyboard. "Ha! I just found an extra bag of plus-ten arrows. Now that the rabid squirrel is dead, we are so killing that big-ass lawn gnome."

"It's a Stone Golem," says Alec.

Huh. Seems the wardrobe conversation is over.

Elle makes shoo-fingers in my direction. "Like I said, take whatever you want!"

"Thanks." Call me shallow, but the thought of raiding Elle's wardrobe has me all smiles. With quick steps, I head into Elle's room and open up her closet. The thing is literally bursting with cool clothes. As I eye the different outfits, I calm down. My wolf slows her incessant pacing.

I pull a little black dress off the hanger. *This will do nicely.* Plus, Elle and I wear the same size shoe. Extra friend bonus.

Stepping over to Elle's full-length mirror, I scan my reflection. I don't like what I see. In some ways, I resemble the same old Bryar Rose: tall and slim with blue eyes and brown hair. Even though I grew up a virtual prisoner in a Manhattan penthouse, I always kept myself relatively put together. My hair stayed styled in neat waves. I put my makeup on just so. If something needed ironing, I did it.

But now? I'm a freaking mess.

Every time I shift, I have to redo everything. Hair. Makeup. Clothes. It's a pain. So right now, the mirror reflects my latest look: frizzed-out hair, no makeup, and an outfit that consists of one of Knox's stolen T-shirts paired with some orange "I heart New York" sweatpants that I picked up at the local bodega for five bucks. Total fashion disaster, but I was desperate and these were all that was left in my size.

I force my spine to straighten. Not to worry. My wardrobe issues will be fixed soon enough. Once Elle and I go fae shopping next week, I can find an enchanted outfit that's unshreddable. Plus, I can handle tonight. I just need to give myself a little verbal pep talk. That means I'll be chatting out loud to myself, but that's my way to coping with stress and I'm sticking to it.

Still staring into the mirror, I launch into my speech. "Tonight will be a super-success. You will not shift in front of all your classmates and then end up naked. There's no chance you'll destroy the hottest new gallery in the Village. And even though the Belvedere has big bay windows, the humans will never see the whole thing and take video on their cell phones."

By the time I'm done with my little speech, my limbs are shaking and my wolf is howling with fear.

That pep talk was crap. I'm more nervous now than ever before.

The sound of a two-tone doorbell echoes into the room, breaking me out of my worries. The barest scent of sandalwood and musk wafts through the air. My insides flutter with excitement.

Knox is here. My inner wolf starts yipping with glee.

I push the intercom button on Elle's wall. "Be right there."

Knox and Alec have an apartment in the same building as me and Elle. One of these days, maybe I'll give him a key, but it's like calling him my mate. I'm just not sure I'm ready for that yet.

Without waiting for a reply over the intercom, I shove on the dress in record time, pull my hair back with a clip, and make for our front door (or as front door as you get in an apartment hi-rise). As I rush to meet Knox, I try giving myself a new pep talk in my mind.

Whatever happens, you can find a way to handle it. You spent most of your life trapped in a penthouse because of your aunties. Now, there's no way you'll stay confined now because of your own fears.

This time, the talk seems to work. As I march toward the front door, my wolf calms and my focus sharpens.

As they say on Broadway, it's showtime.

CHAPTER 2

I whip open the front door. Knox stands in the hallway, his hands in his pockets. I've never seen him in a suit before, and wow, it's a good look on him. The fitted black fabric sets off his dark hair, ice-blue eyes, and tall build. Meanwhile, the scars along his jawline and eyebrow make for a nice contrast to the uptown tailoring.

Knox steps inside, kicks the door closed behind him, and eyes me from head to toe. "You look gorgeous."

"Thanks. So do you?" For some reason, that comes out as a question. I stifle the urge to face-palm myself. Even though Knox and I have been together for a month, I still feel tongue-tied around him.

My wolf has no such issues. Inside my soul, she jumps with glee. *"Our mate has arrived! He's so handsome and smart. Kiss him!"*

"Not feeling it in this moment." I'm more freaked out about tonight, actually.

"But look at his ice-blue eyes and delicious skin. At least, lean in and lick him."

I hug my elbows. My wolf loves to go on and on about how awesome Knox is. Most times, I don't mind. But right now? Her pushing me to kiss Knox is only pushing me to do more things that I don't feel ready for right now. Like the art opening.

Knox's nostrils flare. He's checking out my scent. We weres can tell a lot that way. For instance, if someone's lying, there's always the distinct stink of rotten garbage.

Knox must get a particular smell because he immediately steps inside and pulls me into his arms. His body is firm and warm. I lean in to his chest and inhale his unique scent of sandalwood and musk.

His voice sounds low in my ear. "What's wrong, Bry? Are the dreams back?"

As long as I can remember, I've had dreams of ancient Egypt. Knox has starred in them as well. In these visions, I'm translating papyri about the Book of Isis, the original book of magic. You'd think it would be nice to dream about Egypt, hot guys, and papyri, but there's always a darkness over everything, like something bad's going to happen. Happily, I haven't had the dreams since I started dating Knox.

"No, the dreams aren't back."

"What is it then?"

Right here, this moment. This is what I like so much about being with Knox. He understands me like no one else ever has. I let out a long breath.

"I'm nervous about tonight," I say.

"Your wolf." The way Knox says those two words, it's not a question.

For her part, my wolf is loving all this attention. She leaps and howls with ever increasing levels of joy. *Let's take Knox running with us! A run with Knox... What could be better?*

Knox nuzzles into my neck. "Your wolf talking to you now, isn't she?"

I nod. "She's your biggest fan, you know."

Knox leans back and locks his ice-blue gaze with mine. "What are you afraid of?"

"Shifting in front of my new classmates. Trashing the art opening. Ending up naked and on YouTube tomorrow."

"I get that," says Knox. "So you know, Alec has cast dozens of spells over the Belvedere. Humans won't be able to take a picture of anything."

"That's good. It's just so new, that's all."

Leaning in, Knox presses his forehead against mine. "I understand. Believe me."

The barest hint of lemons fills the air. I smack my lips, trying to place the scent. "You smell…"

Knox leans back and bobs his eyebrows. "Irresistible?"

I chuckle. "No, worried."

"Your sense of smell is getting better. Yeah, I'm worked up."

"So what are you worried about?" My heart pounds a little harder in my chest. Knox is the first guy I've ever kissed, let alone dated. If he's having some kind of emotional issue, I really have no idea what to do here. But I still want to help. That makes it worse.

"It's Az. He wants me to take over as Alpha of the Northeast pack."

Azizi is Knox's father in all but DNA. Plus, Knox is not only a shifter, he's also the warden of all shifter magic, which means he's the strongest of his kind. By rights, Knox should be Alpha of all Alphas, starting with the Northeast pack, which has hundreds of wolves alone. Azizi certainly thinks it's a good idea. But Knox spent a lot of time hunting down our enemies, the Denarii, and the experience made him a bit of a loner. Leading tons of wolves isn't in the cards right now.

I loop my arms around Knox's neck, feeling the cords of muscle slide under my skin. There's something comforting in how solid he is.

"So we both have wolf problems," I say.

"Yeah. But it's good to have someone to share them with."

A sense of warmth and belonging fills my chest. "Same here."

Knox leans in to rub his nose along the length of mine. His barest touch sends shivers through me. "I never felt centered on anything before," he says. "Now, you're the rock in my world. It's a good feeling."

I can't find the words to reply to that, so I go on tiptoe and brush my lips against his. Knox presses me against the wall, his body firm and unyielding against my soft curves. Our kiss deepens. Time seems to stand still until it's only me, Knox, and our kisses. My wolf does this growly-purr noise she makes when she's super-happy. It's one of the few times she and I are in perfect harmony.

Minutes pass before Knox and I speak again.

"Did I mention you look gorgeous?" he asks.

A blush colors my cheeks. "You might have."

"Before we go, I need to know one thing."

"Shoot."

"Do you and Elle have anything special planned for tonight?"

I know exactly what he means. "Elle and I aren't working any schemes tonight."

"Are you sure?"

"Come on." I roll my eyes. "The two of us don't make secret plans all that often, you know."

"Last week, you set an enchanted snake loose in Alec's office."

That's absolutely true. "Please, the little critter wasn't going to hurt anyone. Besides, Alec started it. Mister LeCharme set loose an enchanted mega-spider in our apartment." Like the snake, the spider was totally harmless, but still. Elle and I almost jumped out of our skin when it leapt out of the fridge.

"Nope," says Knox. "The snake was first; the spider was retaliation." Knox and Alec have an apartment down the hallway from me and Elle. It really is too tempting to prank them.

I purse my lips, thinking. "Oh yeah. You're right."

"And before that, you blew up the Denarii League building in Midtown."

"So?"

Knox shakes his head. "I should never have told you that Reggie escaped."

Here's what happened. The Denarii leader, Jules, thought I was going to marry him and become the queen of the zombie-mummy people. As a result, Jules invited every last Denarii in the world to New York to celebrate our wedding. They all showed up except Reggie, who was jailed in the basement of Alec's building. After Jules and his Denarii army were destroyed, Reggie figured it was his time to rise up and become the new zombie-mummy king. He escaped his prison and made for the Denarii's old head-quarters in downtown Manhattan. The Denarii HQ was deserted when we arrived.

I raise my pointer finger. "Hey, Reggie was the one who blew the building up." We're pretty sure that he killed himself in the process, which would be fine with me. More importantly, the explosion didn't hurt any humans, either. "I consider that more of a public service than a scheme."

The flicker of a smile appears on Knox's mouth. "And yesterday, you stole a diamond tiara from Le Charme."

"You know about that?"

In reply, Knox merely lifts his brows. That would be *yes.*

"Sure, we took it. But then, we put it right back. Elle just wanted to be sure her thief skills were still sharp."

This time, Knox only narrows his ice-blue eyes in reply. He really is too cute for words.

"Fine. Elle and I have no schemes planned for tonight."

"Cool." Knox gives me one of his classic chin-nods. "Just keep me posted. I don't want to miss out again."

"Really? I thought for sure you didn't approve of our little projects."

"Are you kidding? I'd have given anything to see Alec with the snake."

My wolf snickers inside my soul. *"It was rather amusing."*

I giggle at the memory. "It really was awesome. We hid the snake in his top desk drawer. After he opened it, Alec ran around his office making yipping noises. That guy has the best scream ever. Elle and I laughed so hard, we both got stomach cramps." My gaze lands on the wall clock. How did it get to be 7:30? "Hey, we should head out."

"Yeah, you're right." Stepping away from me, Knox calls toward the living room. "Are you two ready?"

Alec's voice echoes in to us. "Just one more level."

Knox focuses on me again. "How long has they been gaming?"

"Since last night."

"He's not going anywhere. We better head off solo or we'll miss everything. So you know, Alec has cast dozens of spells over the Belvedere, yeah?"

At the mention of the word *Belvedere*, my inner wolf turns deadly still. That's not good.

I force myself to sound calm. "Yes, it's at the Belvedere."

Knox inhales deeply again. If he catches any change in my scent, he doesn't make a comment. "In that case, let's hit it. Mind if I drive?"

My wolf restarts her pacing and growling routine. *"Ask him to run. RUN!"*

The urge to shift hits me again, hard. It's an effort to keep my fake smile in place. "That sounds like a plan."

In all honestly, I'd go anywhere with Knox. I just hope it doesn't end up with my naked butt going viral on YouTube.

CHAPTER 3

*M*inutes later, Knox and I are tooling through Manhattan in a Mustang. For the record, most weres drive. Confined spaces set off our inner animals, so the subway is a no-go. With a car, you can always pull over if you start to shift. But when you're on a subway train and your wolf goes nuts, people could get hurt. Mostly because they insist on cracking out their cell phones and asking for selfies. I used to wonder at how humans mindlessly expose themselves to danger in exchange for two minutes of social media fame. But then, I think about reality TV. Humans do crazy stuff all the time.

I glance into the rearview mirror. A black pickup truck with tinted windows seems to be following us awfully close. More howlers. Inside the vehicle, I imagine a half-dozen humans are waiting, cell phones in hand, ready to snap pictures of my wolf. I force in a deep breath.

No one is following you, Bry. It's just your imagination.

My wolf disagrees. *"Humans everywhere,"* she growls. *"This is not good."* This time, there's a manic edge to her voice that I've never heard before. Something is seriously wrong.

Knox turns to me. "Your wolf's on edge. What is it?"

I open my mouth, ready to explain how my wolf hates small spaces, but that's not what leaves my lips. Instead, I say something else entirely:

"We're going for a run, mate."

I pop my hands over my mouth. Those words aren't mine. The voice isn't, either.

That was my wolf talking.

I grip Knox's hand. "I didn't mean to say that."

"Got it." Knox pulls an incredibly illegal U-turn in the middle of the Avenue of the Americas. "Change of plans. We're going to the woods."

My shoulders slump with disappointment. "That's probably for the best." Clearly, my wolf isn't ready to meet my classmates. So why does skipping the opening feel like such a failure?

Because I hate to give up, that's why.

Soon we're speeding out of the city. There's no question where Knox is headed. He owns some land up in the Adirondacks. We visit there a lot. It's the perfect spot for shifters. Normally, when we ride to Bear Mountain, we chatter the entire trip. Not so much today, though. As we drive along, silence hangs between us. It seems to take forever to reach Bear Mountain (bear shifters owned the place before Knox got the rights.) Once we arrive, it takes even longer to make the slow march to the main clearing where we usually start our runs.

By the time we're ready to run, the sun hangs low in the sky. Shadows lengthen. Around the clearing, the fir trees stand tall and still. The chitter of insects fills the air. The scent of pine is strong.

We step onto the grassy space. Once we reach the clearing, Knox pauses and turns to me, his face set in serious lines. He pulls off his suit coat and tosses it aside. "We need to settle things, wolf to wolf."

"What do you mean?"

"Back in the car there, your wolf spoke to me. That was a

challenge, both to you and me." Knox starts loosening his tie. "I don't like how your wolf has been acting, making you shift all the time. Even so, I've let it slide because I know she's been cooped up her whole life."

Here's the situation with my wolf. The powerful fairy, Colonel Mallory the Magnificent, cast a spell on me as a baby. It locked down all my power, including my wolf. In fact, I thought I was the variety of Magicorum who didn't have any magic per se, but was just related to someone who did. Long story short, Colonel Mallory did this to save my life. If everyone knew how powerful I really was, I'd have been killed long before I turned seventeen. Even so, the whole experience has my wolf a little twitchy.

Actually, a lot twitchy.

"I've been thinking the same thing," I say. "My wolf has been locked up for so long, all she wants to do is run."

"But your animal is out of control now. You need to give her some structure."

"Our mate is handsome," says my wolf in my head. *"But he talks too much. We need to run now."* The urge to shift moves through me, strong as an electric current.

"Not yet," I reply in my heart. *"We're waiting."*

In reply, my wolf pushes harder against my soul. Fur ripples under my skin. Bands of frustration tighten across my chest. Why can't my wolf just listen?

A muscle feathers in Knox's neck. "Your wolf. She's pushing you now, isn't she?"

My fingers curl with a mixture of helplessness and rage. "No matter what I do, she pops out of my skin anyway."

"That's why packs have Alphas. You need to set her loose, and then, let her attack me."

Every inch of my body goes on alert. "Attack you? Why?"

"Your wolf has been through a lot. Ritual fighting is how wolves work out their place in the pack. Your wolf needs a firm hand."

I stare at my palm. "Firm hand?"

"I'm not talking about physical power here. I'm talking magic. My power is Alpha energy, but you've got your own magic. Once I subdue your wolf, I think you'll get the idea."

My head feels woozy. "Ritual combat? Really?"

"Yes. Release your wolf and attack me. Now."

I hug my elbows. "I'm not sure. If I'm patient, my inner wolf might just calm down on her own."

"That's not how wolves work, even when they aren't of the magical variety. And a werewolf? Our animals are far more intense. I'm your Alpha, and if I let this go on for one more minute, I'm putting you at risk."

Something in his tone sets my nerves on edge. "Meaning?"

"Your wolf will go feral. When it happens, it's fast and intense. Your wolf will take over and you'll disappear."

I suck in a shaky breath. "She wouldn't."

My wolf's voice sounds in my head. *"We will run! I demand we shift NOW!"*

That manic tone to her voice is now higher than ever before. Every inch of my body trembles with the urge to shift. I reply to my wolf in my mind.

"Didn't you hear what Knox said?" Normally, my wolf can't help but listen in on most of my conversations. *"Our mate thinks you're going feral."*

"Mate?" The manic tone to her voice hikes up an octave. *"We have no mate. All we have is the need to run."*

A chill runs up my spine. *"You don't remember our mate?"*

"No mate! Run, now!"

My blood chills. No matter what happens, my wolf always knows her mate. In fact, my usual complaint is that she won't shut up about him.

This is really happening. My wolf is going feral.

All of a sudden, it's like I can't pull in enough air. "You're right. My inner wolf is losing her mind."

"Hey, I won't let that happen." Knox rests his hands on my shoulders. "Breathe, Bry."

It takes serious concentration, but I slow my racing pulse a little. "Okay."

"Now, you need to set your wolf loose and trust me. Can you do that, yeah?"

"I can try."

"Good." Knox pulls off his dress shirt over his head and tosses it aside. "Set her loose."

Normally, the urge to shift is a constant tug of war between me and my wolf. Most times, all it takes is for me to stop fighting the urge to shift. After that, I turn furry. So that's what I do now —I drop my guard and let my wolf take over.

Only, nothing happens.

I speak to my wolf in my mind. *"You can be free now."*

"No fight strange man. I only come out to run."

"What's happening?" asks Knox. "What's your wolf saying?"

I shake my head in disbelief. "She doesn't want to come out."

Knox stalks closer. "It isn't a choice anymore. Your wolf needs to appear. I need to hear you say I can bring her out."

My palms turn slick with sweat. I couldn't stop shifting before, and now I can't start. This simply has to end. And if anyone can help me master this, it's Knox. "Do it."

Knox sets his hands on my shoulders. Waves of power rush through me. Every cell in my body feels charged with energy, only it's not mine. Knox is calling my wolf to appear.

Dots of golden light cloud my vision. My spine twists and lengthens. White fur erupts across my skin. My face becomes a muzzle filled with long white fangs. Yet another cute outfit gets torn to shreds.

I become a wolf.

Light and power surround Knox as well. Golden brightness

shoots out from his skin as he transforms into a giant black wolf. His animal faces mine and speaks. Knox's wolf voice is a basso rumble. "Heed my commands. I'm your Alpha."

All of a sudden, it's like I'm floating outside my wolf-body, watching everything from above. I'm no longer in control; my wolf is. Panic streams through my soul.

It's happened. I've gone feral.

With all my willpower, I struggle to regain control of my body. But when my muzzle opens, it's my wolf who speaks, not me.

"I want to run and be free," my wolf growls at Knox. A frantic gleam shines in her eyes. She still doesn't know Knox is our mate. "I will destroy you if you hinder me."

Those words are like knives—each one cuts into me. It's just like Knox said—when a wolf goes feral, it hits hard and fast. And now, another version of myself is threatening to kill Knox. It's too terrible to be true.

Wolf-Knox replies in a low growl. "You won't kill me."

"I wield all three kinds of magic," continues my wolf. "I can kill anything."

"Raw strength doesn't make you an Alpha."

"Last chance. Let me free or die."

Strangely enough, some small part of me actually feels sorry for my wolf. The way my wolf looks and talks? She truly is losing her mind. On the other hand, more of me is terrified that I'll spend the rest of my life hovering over my own wolfish form, completely powerless.

Go get her, Knox.

Wolf-Knox digs in his front paws, lowers his head, and bares his teeth. "Do. Your. Best."

I watch in horror as my wolf-self lunges at Wolf-Knox. From my floating spot above the fray, I watch our animals war it out— one white and one black against a backdrop of green grass. Wolf-Knox moves first. He leaps in, pinning my wolf to the ground.

My animal rakes her claws along Wolf-Knox's belly. He roars and flinches. The movement is enough of a break for my wolf. She kicks Wolf-Knox off her. My mate goes flying across the field, his claws digging into the soil to stop the force of the throw. A long line of torn-up grass opens in his wake.

From my perch in the sky, I watch the fight in terror. My body may feel numb, but my soul is a raw nerve of worry. My wolf is crazy-strong. What if she hurts Knox?

Wolf-Knox turns around and charges at my wolf. She crouches low on her front paws, getting ready for the eventual attack. At the last moment, Wolf-Knox leaps into the air. He's a blur of black power as he whips over my white wolf's prone form. A moment later, Wolf-Knox lands behind my wolf, taking out her back legs with a great swipe of his front paws. The air around the two shimmers with power.

Knox's Alpha energy.

My wolf gets flipped onto her back. Wolf-Knox leaps atop her. In a fluid motion, he has his canines set against my wolf's throat.

"Relent," he growls.

A long moment follows while my wolf pauses, considering what to do next. The vibrations of Alpha power turn more intense. The area around Wolf-Knox and my animal starts to vibrate, reminding me of heat waves rolling off asphalt on a summer day.

My wolf shivers as the tension leaves her body. I know the moment when she gives in to the magic. "I relent, my mate."

And then, I feel.

The waves of Knox's Alpha power move through me again, warming my soul and strengthening my resolve. A heartbeat later, I find myself pulled back inside my own wolf-body. I'm on my back, my hind claws scraping across Wolf-Knox's abdomen. Knox doesn't budge. I'm pinned, end of story. Immediately, I relax my legs and expose my own neck. It's the wolf way to show submission. The fight is over.

Wolf-Knox nuzzles into me, speaking in a low grumble. "That's my Bry."

"I never want to go feral again." Searching my soul, I check on my wolf. She's exhausted and barely conscious.

"Mate," whispers my wolf. *"We're with our mate."*

Usually, I feel a little strange when my wolf calls Knox our mate, but this time? It sounds pretty awesome. *"That's right. Knox is our mate."*

Wolf-Knox tilts his head. "How's your animal?" he asks.

"Ready for a nap. Can she fall asleep while I'm all furry?"

"Sure, if you want her to. You chose this form."

I lean my head back into the grass. "No, I didn't. You chose it for me."

"I'm just showing you how it's done. Did you feel the magic flow from me into you? Next time, you need to do that inside yourself, sending your own magic into your wolf. You've got a lot more power inside you than I do. You can do this, Bry. Set loose all three kinds of magic."

"The last time I set all my magic loose, I killed Jules. It's not safe." A lead weight of worry settles into my stomach. Some days, I feel like a ticking bomb, ready to blow away everyone around me and powerless to know how to control the explosion.

"It feels unsafe because you aren't used to it. But you'll get there. You've got strength of heart, Bry." He nuzzles into my neck once more. "That's what's most important."

For a hot second, everything feels right in the world. "Keep telling me that, and one day I might believe it."

"You've discovered my master plan." Knox leaps aside and starts trotting off toward the trees.

I hop back onto all four paws. "Where are you going?"

"For a run, of course."

"What about the art opening? I should meet the other students from West Lake."

Knox's eyes flare with golden light. "You'll meet them soon enough. I almost lost you back there. Right now, I don't want to share you with anyone."

Once Knox speaks the words, I realize they are true for me as well. "Race you to the woods."

"That's my Bry."

I take off for the tree line as fast as my paws can carry me. The night deepens. An owl hoots. Knox races along beside me. I've never felt more loved and free.

CHAPTER 4

*I*t's close to midnight by the time Knox and I finish our run. All too soon, we've both returned to our human forms and are driving back to the city. Knox keeps extra clothes on his property for when he shifts, but I go through mine at a much faster rate than he does. Right now, I'm wearing a pair of his gym shorts—which I have to hold on to with one hand or they fall down—and a black T-shirt that comes down to my knees.

Plus, I like wearing Knox's stuff. It smells like him. That might be wolfy of me, but what can I say? I am a were, after all.

Still, it'd be nice to have my own stuff too. Elle and I really need to finalize our plans about going fae shopping. I can't spend the rest of my life looking like a slob, not to mention the amateur paparazzi issue. Nothing says *I'm a werewolf* like walking around Manhattan barefoot in ill-fitting clothes with leaves stuck in your hair. I might as well wear a sign that says *"Magicorum selfies here."*

My gaze locks again on the rearview mirror. It might be my imagination, but is that the same black pickup truck that I saw before we left the city?

"Hey, Knox?"

"What's up?"

I gesture toward the mirror, but the pickup truck is gone. "I thought I saw someone following us."

"What did the—" Knox's cell phone starts beeping like crazy. "One sec." He pulls the device out of a cup holder and checks the screen. "Damn. It's a text from Az. Something's up at Lucky's bar. Mind if we take a detour?"

"Not at all."

All thoughts of the pickup truck disappear from my mind. Azizi is not only Knox's honorary father, he's an old were who grows weaker by the day. Magic is all about balance. Azizi is the previous shifter warden. Knox is the new one. As Knox grows more powerful, Azizi moves closer to death.

"Did the text say what's going on?" I ask.

"No, just to head over to Lucky's ASAP." Lucky's bar is a were-only place. Azizi lives in one of the back rooms of Lucky's bar. Knox grips the steering wheel more tightly. "Damn, I hope he's okay." He glances at his phone again. "And now his phone is off."

A chill settles over my skin. Az usually stays in his wolf form, so he rarely turns his phone on, let alone uses it. In fact, it's something that makes Knox a little crazy. Az never calls Knox to ask for anything, even if he needs a healer or food. Azizi is all old school. No tech. No help. That makes this text super-weird.

Knox eyes me carefully. "On second thought, maybe I should take you home first. I have no idea what we're getting into."

My rebel-reflex kicks in. "I'm going. And after what just happened, you know I'm good in a fight."

A small smile rounds Knox's full mouth. "That you are."

We turn down a side street in Brooklyn, and there it is: a beat-up wooden house on a street corner lined with other beat-up wooden houses. There's a small sign reading *"Lucky's"* and a flight of stairs going underground. Normally, there's no one near the place. Not so tonight.

The place is overrun with humans.

They stand in a long line down the darkened street: men, women, and even kids. All of them have cameras and expectant looks on their faces. As we tool up to the curb, a hundred cells lift in our direction. Voices echo through the night.

"They might be weres."

"Get it on video."

"Mommy, you promised to show me a real-life werewolf."

In my opinion, that last comment was the ultimate in crazy. Seriously, who thinks it's a good idea to drag their kid to a bar in Brooklyn to see a werewolf? I scan the line of humans.

A lot of parents, evidently.

Knox kills the engine. This particular stretch of curb isn't a legal parking spot, but we don't have time to find a garage. The mustang's windows are tinted. We can see out, but the humans can't see in. And based on what I see outside? This scene has all the makings of a disaster. Lucky's is a were-only club for a reason. The shifters who come here do not want to interact with humans.

Knox thumps his palm on the steering wheel. "Damn, there are weres at Lucky's with a serious vendetta against humans. This could push them over the edge."

I lean over and grip his wrist. "You stopped me. You can help them, too."

At this point, I don't know what's more surprising: the fact that Lucky's is overrun with humans or that Knox knows so much about his fellow weres. Knox has been really clear that he doesn't want to be Alpha over anyone. Looks like he's keeping an eye on some of his fellow weres anyway.

"Let's hit it." Knox and I step out onto the sidewalk, and the place erupts. Everywhere, folks are shouting for us to take a picture or tell us if we're really werewolves. Someone tosses a silver dollar at my face while shouting at me to tell them if I'm allergic to silver. A woman in some kind of robe chants in a made-up language while spraying lavender perfume in the air. All the while, she asks for my wolf to come out.

Thankfully, my wolf is still happily zonked out inside me, or she'd definitely freak out and shift at this scene. I hightail it toward the main door of Lucky's. The bouncer is a big guy—should be; he's a werewolf. Knox pulls me against his side as he addresses the bouncer. "What's up, Gage?"

"Wards stopped working," says Gage. "I've never seen anything like it."

"How's Azizi?" I ask. "Is he all right?"

"Not all right," replies Gage. "More like amped to the max. The old wolf is calling for war. You two need to see him. Calm him down if you can." Gage shoves open the door. A wave of music, voices, and smells pours out onto the street. Knox and I wave to Gage as we shove our way into the crowded space. Lucky's was always a snug space filled with lots of high-tops and a long wooden bar, but it's never felt more crowded than it has now. Even with our extra shifter strength, it seems to take forever for me and Knox to reach the back wall.

Humans cluster around anyone oversized and gruff looking, figuring they must be a were. Unfortunately, they're spot on. A few have cameras on selfie sticks and are narrating their own YouTube channels.

"Smile at the nice wolf-man while Mommy takes your picture."

"Can you believe this, viewers? I've found an actual shifter bar right here in Brooklyn."

In terms of the werewolves, they're standing frozen in place, looking shell-shocked or ready to rip out the nearest throat. This situation has seconds left before some bad stuff happens.

In the far corner, there's a door that leads to Azizi's room. It's been ripped off its hinges. Humans have jammed themselves into the hallway. Some are drinking. Others laughing. More seem to be pounding on the doors, asking for the weres inside to "come out and play."

My breath catches. Azizi is behind one of those doors. I saw what that old were did to the army of zombie-mummies. He may look old, but Azizi can still kill with the best of them when his blood is up.

Those humans really don't want him to come out and play.

Knox and I share a quick look. I can scent the worry and rage simmering on him; the smell of burning charcoal seeps from his pores. His wolf is close to the surface as well. Hints of golden light flicker in Knox's eyes. Not good. If the humans see that, we'll never get close to Azizi. Knox will get swarmed for sure. And then? I shudder.

Fortunately, while Knox's wolf is ready to appear, mine is still konked out. I don't think we could handle this if both of us were ready to shift. I link my fingers with his. "Follow me."

Pulling on Knox's arm, I guide him through the crowded hallway. I may stomp toes and bump shoulders along the way, but this is New York. If you can't handle jostling in a crowd, move somewhere else.

Soon we reach Azizi's door. Knox tries to open it, but the old were is leaning against the wood. The door will open an inch or two, enough to reveal a wall of gray fur. That's definitely Azizi.

"It's us, Azizi!" I yell. "Knox and Bry. Let us in."

The door opens a crack. Part of a grizzled human face is visible through the shadows. I've never seen Azizi as anything but a wolf before. Now I can tell that his human side has cocoa-dark skin, a deeply lined face, and a shock of grey hair atop his head. He scans Knox and me for a moment before speaking.

"Come in."

Knox and I slip into the room. Like always, the place looks pretty bare: concrete floor, no furniture. By the time we enter, Az has already shifted back to his wolf form. Instead of a grizzled old human, now a massive gray animal stalks the floor. For his part, Knox takes up Az's old position of leaning against the doorway to keep the humans out.

Az's fur is standing on edge and his eyes are golden bright. "Thank you for coming. I need help getting these fools out of my den. If I go out there, I'll tear them apart."

"You can call me anytime." Behind Knox's back, the door shimmies as humans try to open it. "What happened to the wards, Az?"

"You must find the fountain. Magic is changing."

The fountain part is nothing new. There are wardens for all three kinds of magic: were, warlock, and fairy. Knox is the warden for shifters; Alec has that job for witches and warlocks. We don't know who's the warden for the fae, but all three of them are supposed to be guarding the fountain of magic. Trouble is, no one knows where the fountain is. My hobby—okay, it's more of an obsession—is translating the Book of Isis to try to find the fountain. In fact, I've spent years dreaming about ancient Egypt and translating ancient papyri, all of it about the Book of Isis. So the fountain part isn't new. The other stuff is a revelation, though.

"What do you mean, magic is changing?" I ask Az.

"The wards were strong. They simply changed from wards to beacons. Attracted humans instead of repelled them."

Alec placed about a dozen warding spells here to keep humans away from Lucky's. There are castings to hide the building, cause irrational fear to anyone who gets close, you name it. To human eyes, they look like regular rocks on the sidewalk.

"That doesn't make sense," says Knox. "Alec is a strong wizard. I've never seen one of his spells fail."

"Not fail," corrects Az. "Flip. All magic is changing now."

Knox and I share a long look. If magic is changing, it probably means something not good for the wardens who guard it. "How does this affect Knox?" I ask.

Az finally pauses from his nonstop pacing. "I don't know. I

can't think with all these humans around. I must get these fools out of my den."

"We're on it," says Knox.

Az sits and tilts his massive head. "You stop it," growls Az. "I need to speak with Bryar Rose. Alone."

Knox and I exchange another long look. His scent changes again; this time, it has the acidic tang of worry. "I'll be fine," I say. "Clear out the humans before trouble starts."

"No police," warns Az. "They keep lists of shifter dens. This is my home, not some animal preserve."

"Right." Knox pulls his cell from his pocket and punches a few buttons. "Hey, Alec. I need a favor. Lucky's is overrun with humans. I need you get over here and help me clear the place out before I kill anyone. Oh, and you have to cast some new wards... No, I don't know what happened to the last set of spells. Az says magic is changing. You need to up your game here." Knox listens for a minute, then focuses on Az. "Alec wants to know if wrapping his new wards in solidity spells will help them stick around."

"Solidity spells." Az narrows his golden eyes. "Yes, that should work."

Knox speaks into his phone once more. "Az says solidity spells should do it, so get over here... What? No, I don't care if you're still playing Kazimir's Gate with Elle. Transport your lazy ass to Lucky's." He pushes End Call and jams the phone in his pocket. "That guy makes me crazy sometimes."

"He likes to push your buttons," I say. Knox and Alec have been friends since they were kids. Alec has made teasing Knox into a kind of art form.

All of a sudden, a bright orb of red light appears inside the room. Warlock magic. I wince, covering my eyes with my forearm as the brightness grows and takes the form of two people. With a final burst of red light, the spell ends.

Alec and Elle are here. On a side note, I'm glad to see that they've both showered and changed since I last saw them. Now they both wear jeans and long henleys. As always, Alec has paired his look with a sports coat. No doubt, the thing is packed with wizard gemstones. Alec thinks that man-bags of stones only advertise you're a wizard, and he likes to keep his skills secret.

Az lifts his chin. "Good to see you, wizard." He then focuses on Elle. "And the ward of Blackaverre. Welcome."

Blackaverre is Elle's fairy godmother. Turns out, Az has been around hundreds of years and knows pretty much everybody and everything. That's how he could tell if the solidity spell would work.

Knox glares at Alec. "Thanks for making time."

"Always." Alec winks. "It seems you have a human problem." Alec reaches into his pocket and pulls out a handful of gems. "All I need to do is cast a few spells. Fear, extra speed, loss of memory. That way, they'll want to go and not remember a thing about this place. That ought to do it."

"And I'll use my powers, too," adds Elle. "I'll ask them to leave, not come back, and forget the place existed. Only I use my natural charm, not magic." She winks at Alec. His tanned face reddens.

"Will that work?" asks Knox.

"Elle is fae," I explain. "Part of her magic is that she can convince anyone to do pretty much anything."

"Sound good," says Knox. "And I'll usher people out the door and try not to kill anyone." He focuses on me. "How about you?"

"Bryar Rose will stay and keep me company," says Az.

My brows lift. "I will?" Az has never asked to spend time alone with me before.

Knox's stance stiffens. I can scent his protectiveness from across the room. "What's wrong, Az?"

"This is for Bryar Rose alone." Az has a deep voice that says, *I mean business.*

Knox focuses on me. "Are you cool with that?"

"I'm fine," I say. "Go clean out Az's den."

It doesn't take long for Alec, Elle, and Knox to leave the room and get to work. Within seconds, the noise of human voices and overloud music starts to die down. My friends are clearing out the bar without too much trouble. In fact, the humans even stop pounding on the door to Az's room. I cross the floor to kneel beside him.

"What's going on, Az?"

He shifts his massive wolf's head to focus right at me. "Tell me about these dreams of yours. The ones of Ancient Egypt."

Shock prickles across my skin. "How do you know about that?"

Azizi chuckles. "I know a lot of things. Let's just say being alive for hundreds of years has its advantages." His voice lowers. "Tell me about your dreams."

"I see ancient Egypt, a room full of papyri, and Knox. But I haven't had them since I shifted a month ago and starting dating Knox. Why? Should I still be having them?"

"Yes. In them you'll see the Void, an ancient being. As magic rises again, so does the Void to swallow it up."

The Void. That can't be good.

"Maybe I have seen any strange figure in my dreams. What does the Void look like?"

"I was hoping you could tell me." Az moves to lie down, resting his muzzle on the concrete floor. "If you saw him, you'd know. The Void is a fearsome enemy."

His words make my hair stand on end. "I thought I was done with the fearsome enemy thing. Wasn't fighting Jules bad enough? That guy was king of the zombie-mummies."

"Jules? He was nothing." Az huffs out a breath. "You're getting stronger. As you grow in power, so do the Void's followers."

"The Void's followers? Do you mean there are more zombie-mummies?"

"My sources tell me that the Denarii are gone now."

"All of them? Do you know if we got Reggie?"

Az squints. "Who was he?"

"Reggie was this nutty Denarii that Knox had locked up in the basement of Alec's office building."

"That Denarii." Az nods slowly. "The one who escaped."

"That's the one. Is he dead?"

Az sniffs. "If my sources say all the Denarii are dead, then that means Reggie as well."

I wince. Somehow, that answer doesn't feel as comforting as it should.

"We don't have time for the Denarii," continues Az. "The followers of the Void are the Shadowvin. They are creatures of ancient magic who are returning to our world."

The hairs on the back of my neck stand on end. "What does that mean?"

"You haven't had the dream of the Void yet. He possesses ancient magic. That power will wipe away every word I've said until the Void deems the time to be right. Keep translating papyri. When you meet the Void in your dreams, you'll remember this conversation."

"I'm going to forget talking to you?" I wince. It doesn't seem real.

"The moment you step out into the hallway, yes." Azizi sighs. "In any case, after you dream, you will start to remember. When that happens, come see me. I'll do what I can to help."

"Thank you." The Void and the Shadowvin…it all seems too awful to be true.

A loud crash sounds from inside the bar. "I better go check on my friends," I tell Az. "Thank you again for everything."

Az closes his eyes. "Until you dream again," he says in his low voice.

I leave the room and step out into the now-deserted hallway. As I pass over the threshold to Az's room, a flash of white light fills my vision. An arctic chill crawls across my skin, like thousands of frozen needles pushing into me at once.

Magic is at work.

For a moment, my head feels as white and empty as the light around me. After that, the hallway returns to normal. I scrub my hands over my face. There was something important that Azizi was telling me, but it all seems like a dream now.

The memory feels just out of reach, and then it disappears entirely.

I step around in a slow circle. What was I doing here again? I check on my inner animal, but she's still konked out after the battle with Knox.

That thought kicks my mind back into gear. I'm here with Knox to help Az from the humans.

Speaking of which, where are the humans anyway? The hallway is deserted. The humans are gone. I'm about to check on Azizi one last time when Elle steps into the hallway.

"What was that crashing?" I ask.

"Now that the mortals took off, the weres are fighting one another. That's pretty typical." Elle steps closer. "What did Az talk to you about?"

"He asked me about my dreams and then...I mean..." I shake my head. For some reason, I can't recall anything after that. I'm about to ask Elle what that means when I hear more crashing from the main bar, followed by the low whisper of a high-pitched female voice.

"Knox is mine."

With my new were senses, I can hear the possessiveness and rage echoing through the strange woman's voice. My inner wolf, who'd been fast asleep after her fight with Knox, perks right up. Any thoughts about discussing my conversation with Az disappear.

"Our mate is being claimed by another," my wolf growls. *"He is ours!"*

A surge of primal energy moves through me. My wolf is right.

Knox is my mate and no one else's. My hands clench into fists as I take off toward the bar. Elle follows along behind me.

"What's wrong?" she asks. "Your eyes have gone all golden."

"Someone is talking about Knox."

"I didn't hear anything."

"You wouldn't," I say. "It's a wolf thing." I kick open the door to the main bar, and then I see it. Some were girl in an all-denim outfit who's draped across Knox.

And she's kissing him.

I've never been angrier in my life. Neither has my wolf.

Whatever happens next, one thing is certain.

I'm ready for a fight.

CHAPTER 5

*F*or the record, Knox told me about the particular werewolf who's now hanging off his face. Her name's Joy. I've never met her before, but Joy looks exactly how Knox described her.

Big hair.

All-denim outfit.

Strong sense of entitlement.

Oh, Joy.

The topic of Joy came up when Knox and I were sharing our dating history. My side of the conversation was short; I'd only ever kissed Knox. For his part, Knox has dated a lot. As a warden, Knox didn't think he could take a mate, so he overcompensated with dating. And considering how Knox travelled the world killing Denarii, my guy had a lot of opportunities to date. Joy was on the no-dating list because the first time they smooched, she didn't so much kiss Knox as over-lick his face. *Ick.*

I scan the bar, trying not to focus on how Knox keeps pushing Joy away and she keeps not getting the hint. About a dozen guys wait along the walls. Based on their scents, all of them are weres in their human forms. Elle and Alec stand by the front door near the bouncer, Gage.

No one is talking.

All eyes seem to be on me.

My limbs tremble with rage.

A tiny voice in my head—presumably my human side—reminds me that I should be gracious, wait for Knox to scrape Joy off, and then saunter out the front door with my man, Hollywood style. But then, Joy licks Knox's ear.

That voice doesn't stand a chance.

I am so pounding this girl into the floor.

"Set me loose," croons my inner wolf. *"I'll tear out her throat and quickly."*

White-hot fury heats my veins. My wolf form tears out of me, and I do zero to stop it. Within seconds, I'm huge, white, furry, and out of my mind with rage. I dash across the room, bite into Joy's shoulder, and tear her off my mate. She skids across the floor and then hops up to stand. We weres are quick healers. Whatever bite mark I made on her shoulder is already gone.

"What are you, crazy?" Her poufy hair now has a flat spot on the side of her head—that's from where I threw her across the floor. It's an improvement.

"I am Knox's mate," I growl.

That gets a big reaction. Half the room gasps, which isn't surprising. Very few werewolves can speak.

"But Knox is mine…" stammers Joy. "And you…"

I claw the wood flooring with my right front paw. *Scrrrratch.*

"Leave now or I'll get angry," I warn.

Knox saunters to my side. "Look, Joy. I've vowed not to fight your pack. But Bry here? Not so much."

When I speak again, my voice is a low rumble. "This is the part where you leave."

Joy doesn't need to be told twice. She races for the front door, shoving Gage out of the way as she speeds toward the street.

The moment Joy's gone, all the rage seeps from my body. My wolf, who'd been exhausted before, becomes downright catatonic. It's not so much a thought as a reflex when I shift back. My body shrinks. Bones realign. All fur vanishes.

I'm becoming human again.

And naked.

In a room full of strange weres. Welcome to my personal nightmare.

Luckily, Knox thinks quickly. He grabs a checkerboard tablecloth from a nearby high-top. As I shift forms, Knox wraps it around me like a sheet. In this moment, I've never been happier for his quick reflexes.

Once I finish shifting, I pull the cloth more tightly around my shoulders. For the first time, I really scan the male weres around me. There are no females other than Joy, but that's not surprising. Girl weres are really rare. In terms of the guy weres, it's a mix of ages, but some of the younger guys seem familiar.

"Don't I know you from somewhere?" I ask.

"We're not Knox's pack, if that's what you're asking," says one guy. He's got gorgeous shoulder-length blond hair. It's really impressive, considering how I know for a fact that he can't use product. Shifting and styling solutions don't mix.

I shake my head. "That wasn't what I was asking." Next to the guy with the awesome hair, there's a teenager with unruly dark locks and big ears. I scan him carefully. "You look familiar, too."

He waves at me. "I'm Abe and I'm not pack, either." He gestures to the guy beside him. "This here's Hollywood. So you know, the only weres that Knox connects with are you and him. Not us. That sucks because Knox is a warden." He kicks at the floor. "He'd be a great Alpha."

"Abe," growls Knox. "The warden thing is supposed to be secret."

"Why?" asks Hollywood. "You're the only massive black wolf

with an Alpha aura that I can sense a mile away. And Bry here is clearly your mate."

Knox pinches the bridge of his nose. "Even more personal stuff."

"If you made us pack, then it wouldn't matter." The way Abe is talking, this is clearly a major disappointment in his life. A memory appears. Az wants Knox to lead of the Northeast pack. I'm guessing these guys are some of those wolves.

Hollywood tosses his head, making his golden locks shimmer in the bar light. "We look familiar? We were some of the wolves who saved you from that zombie army." He taps his chest. "We risked our lives. Now by rights, we should be pack."

Knox shakes his head. "Az said you helped of your own free will. Bry and I owe you nothing."

I look to Knox. "Maybe I should head back to the apartment and get dressed. It's been a long day. And honestly, this is a super-awkward conversation, especially when you're wrapped in a tablecloth."

Abe gives me pleading looks. It's as if it were a hot summer day and I was holding the last ice cream cone in the universe. "Don't you think we should be pack?"

I clear my throat. Werewolf life rules are something I know zero about. "Well…I don't know…"

Knox wraps his arm protectively around my shoulder. "You better get going. This is between me, Abe, and Hollywood."

"If you say so." It's an effort not to make eye contact with Abe. He really knows how to work those *give me some ice cream* eyes.

"You've had a big day, Bry. You look exhausted. " Knox glances over to Alec and raises his voice. "You transport Bry and Elle, yeah?"

Alec nods. "Sure thing."

Going up on tiptoes, I give Knox a quick peck goodbye. After that, I speed-walk over to Elle and Alec. Turns out, it's really nerve-racking to walk around with nothing but a tablecloth to hide your nakedness.

Knox is still grumbling with Abe and Hollywood. I move to stand behind Elle, using her body as a shield.

"Did you see my butt at all?" I whisper.

"Nope, you're fine." Elle shoots me a thumbs-up. "And nice wolf control there, by the way."

"She wanted out and I let her; that's not really control yet." Disappointment weighs onto my shoulders.

My inner wolf rouses from her half-sleep. *"I still should have torn out her throat."*

"Noted," I reply.

Across the bar, Knox and the two weres keep grumbling away at each other. I catch the words "Denarii" and "buzz off." Knox is the gruff one, while Abe and Hollywood are still looking pleading and pathetic. In fact, they look so miserable, I'm tempted to walk across the room and ask Knox to rethink the whole pack thing. I mean, I have no idea what it means, but these two guys did try to save my life. Who cares if they want to be part of our group of friends?

I'm about to step back to Knox when Alec pulls a few gems from the pocket of his sport coat. "Let's get you ladies home."

For a second, I consider passing on returning to the apartment so I can chat with Knox, Abe, and Hollywood. But then I realize it's very possible that my left ass cheek is hanging out in the breeze. Time to get out of here.

Gripping the stones in his hand, Alec closes his eyes. An electric sense of magic fills the air. Sometimes with warlock power, the energy vibrates through my body until it feels like my teeth are coming loose. Within seconds, tendrils of red cloud swirl around our feet, marking out the three of us for a spell. Waves of magic tingle across my skin. My stomach flutters, and that's when I know the spell has started.

We're being magically transported home.

When the smoke clears, Elle and I are back in our apartment. Alec reaches into his pocket once more. "If you don't mind, I'll transport back to Lucky's. Knox has it all under control, but I'm still his wingman."

I narrow my eyes at Alec. "You think there could be trouble with Abe and Hollywood? They seemed pretty harmless."

"No trouble." Alec chuckles. "I like watching Knox grump at someone else for a change."

"Right." I can't help but smile as well. I forgot how Knox is basically Mister Grouchy to everyone else besides me. I'm the only one who gets to see his cuddly side, and I like it that way.

We say our goodbyes, and Alec casts yet another transport spell. Within seconds, he's gone. The moment me and Elle are alone again, I reposition my tablecloth for the umpteenth time. A blob of ketchup and some kind of brown goo is now smeared across my right boob. That does it. This werewolf-wardrobe situation has officially gone too far.

I turn to Elle. "You know how we planned to go fae shopping next week?"

Elle eyes my nasty tablecloth-toga. The thing smells like old ketchup and fryer grease. "You wanted to get an unshreddable outfit."

"Think we can go tomorrow?"

Elle grins from ear to ear. "Oh, yeah." She notices some tooth puncture marks on my shoulder. They're almost healed now, but there's a slight redness still. I'll get better at the healing thing the longer I'm a wolf. Until then, nothing looks like werewolf bite. Elle's face slackens with shock. "Hey, what happened to you?"

"Knox may have driven me out to the woods and asked me to kill him with my wolf."

Elle takes a half-step backward. "What?"

"My wolf had been getting out of control. It's an animal thing. Knox needed to show her who was in charge and show me how to do it as well. I don't have Alpha power, but there's a ton of other magic in here." I tap my chest. "Knox thinks I have more than enough to control her."

"That's great!" Elle beams. "I know it's been bothering you how you can't control your wolf. Has Knox's advice helped?"

"My wolf has been borderline catatonic since the fight, so I don't know yet." I shift my weight from foot to foot. It's good to know my wolf can be controlled by magic, but I still don't know how to make it work.

"All the more reason to go to bed early and let me get things ready. Here's the deal. Fairies don't like weres. They don't like warlocks. They really don't even like other fairies. If we're going to go shopping, you need to get a handle on your animal. That wolf pops out, and we're kicked out of the store for good. And probably cursed. Oh, and murdered in some slow and painful way." Elle winces. "Fairies. They are all things cruel and horrible in a cute package."

"Say no more. I'm heading to bed." I sniff the stinky tablecloth. "You know, after I shower."

"Good plan."

As I trudge off to the bathroom, I try to ignore the jittery feeling in my chest at the thought of fae shopping. Sure, fairies hate everyone, but all Elle and I need to do is get one unshreddable outfit. I'm sure my wolf can behave for a few hours.

Pretty sure.

Maybe sure.

I picture Queen Nyxa, the fairy who joined my last birthday party. She enjoyed enchanting mortals into dancing themselves to death. And that was when she was in a good mood. The thought sends a chill up my spine.

It takes an effort, but I'm able to shake thoughts of Nyxa from my mind.

Tomorrow will be fine. There's nothing to worry about. Hopefully.

CHAPTER 6

*T*he next morning, I wake up to the sight of my boyfriend Knox. He leans over my bed, wearing a leather jacket and a sly grin. There are a number of things I could say at this moment.

How did you get into our apartment?

Why are you here at 7 a.m.?

Do I smell bagels?

Instead, I say the most important thing first: "Elle and I are going fae shopping today."

Knox lifts his brows. "I didn't know they were for sale."

"They're not, but they have their own network of hidden stores in Manhattan." I lace my fingers behind my head. "Remember how you wanted to know about the next big scheme for me and Elle?"

"I did."

"This is it. Fae shopping." And because I just woke up and am not yet thinking clearly, I move right on to the second most important order of business. "Thank you for bringing me bagels."

One advantage of being a werewolf is you have an incredible sense of smell.

"I did, yeah." Knox runs his finger along my jawline. "Alec is bringing the lox and stuff."

At the sound of Alec's name, Elle's voice echoes in from her room. These walls are like paper. "Did Knox say Alec is coming?"

"That he did. He'll be here any second with lox."

Elle whips open my bedroom door. "Good morning, Bry. I let Knox in. Is Alec coming over?"

Knox does his chin-nod thing. "Yup."

"Do I look terrible?" she asks. "I'm not a morning person." Elle isn't lying. Her hair is knotted into one of those beehive things that went out in the 1960's. It really is amazing the kind of bedhead she achieves.

No point making Elle feel crappy about her bedhead, though. "Who looks great in the morning?"

"Runway models," says Elle. "Most of lower Manhattan."

Okay, she has me there.

"You look adorable. I love those jammies." Today, Elle is wearing these super-cute flannel pajamas with little cartoon tigers all over them. Adorable.

"Really?" She smooths down the top. "Well, I'm not leaving them on just to look cute for Alec."

I'm aiding her self-delusion, but what else are friends for? "Okay, but no boys when we go fae shopping."

Knox gives me a chin nod. "That's right. Fae don't like weres." His ice-blue eyes narrow. "Will you be safe?"

"Bry has fairy power," explains Elle. "So I can sneak her into stores. But having you along? Nuh-uh." She twiddles her fingers at us. "I'll let you discuss." With that, Elle leaves the room.

Knox frowns. "I'm not too crazy about you going shopping at stores run by the fae. I can wait outside or whatever."

I crook my finger at Knox. He leans in closer. "Here's the thing, big guy."

Knox runs his nose along the length of mine. That move always makes my insides go squirmy. "Yeah?"

"Most of my schemes with Elle are dangerous."

"I get it." Knox brushes a kiss across my lips. "You two don't need a babysitter. Just promise me one thing."

"What?"

"Keep your cell handy. Text me TBL for trouble. That way, I'll know to come running."

"TBL. You got it."

"Cool." A faraway look washes over Knox's ice-blue eyes. I don't know Knox too well yet, but I've seen that face before. It's the one he wears sometimes when we say goodbye.

"What are you up to today?"

"I need to see Az again."

My brows lift. "Is everything at Lucky's okay?"

"Oh, the place is fine now. Alec put in new wards last night. They seem to be holding." Knox sighs. "Nope, the trouble is that Az wants to have another talk with me. About leading."

"Those two weres—Abe and Hollywood—they're part of the Northeast pack, aren't they?"

"Yeah. And they're really persistent." Knox sits down on the bed. "I'm just not ready to lead. Before you, Alec was my only friend. And I rarely saw him. Most of my time was spent hunting and killing Denarii. Being pack means being connected to other weres 24-7. They'll get in both of our heads in a way that can't be undone. It's a huge commitment. I can't even look at them without wanting to run."

I link my fingers with his. "There's no rush to be pack Alpha. But maybe there's a step between being mentally connected and growling at them?"

Knox gives me a crooked smile. "I don't growl that much."

I give his hand a squeeze. "You're a total grouch and I like it that way. I don't like sharing your sweet side with anyone."

"Mmm." Knox grins, leans in, and brushes a gentle across my lips. "That's enough about Az and pack politics. Tell me, what are you shopping for, exactly?"

I must be getting better at this girlfriend thing, because I can tell that Knox isn't ready to talk any more about the situation with Az. "We're getting some girl stuff. You know."

"Like enchanted tampons or something?"

"I can't believe you just said the words *enchanted tampons*." I punch him in the shoulder.

"Go on. You can tell me anything. Even the enchanted tampon thing, yeah?"

Knox's eyes look especially big, blue, and earnest. He really would talk tampons with me if I needed it. But I don't. "Well, you know how when we shift into our wolf forms, we all end up naked?"

"Yeah. I told you; it's not a big thing for weres."

"Well, I wasn't raised to be a werewolf, and it's super-awkward for me, especially because there aren't a lot of girl weres."

Knox rubs his neck. "I can see where you're going with this."

"So Elle and I are going shopping for some enchanted clothes that I won't destroy when I shift. I'll feel more comfortable then, especially at West Lake Prep."

"That's cool." Knox tilts his head. "Why didn't you tell me before?"

"I thought it might be insulting to were culture or something."

"Hey, I don't want to look at some stranger's junk any more than the next person. What are you thinking about?"

I scooch in closer. This is shopping talk, so I need to be able to focus. "Maybe some jeans and a top. What do people wear at West Lake Prep?"

"Regular stuff, I guess. I can't get a straight answer out of Alec." He bobs his brows up and down. "Yet."

We've talked about this a few times. Alec's family is on the board of West Lake Prep. For the record, I was super-excited to attend this school because it seemed like the perfect normal school. Well, normal for parts of Manhattan anyway. Alec pulled some strings to get me, Knox, and Elle to attend for our senior year. I'm super happy to be attending, but I need to get my wolf under control. Reading school brochures can wait for later.

An idea appears. "Hey, when I'm at the store, do you want me to pick up something for you?"

"Sure, that's a great idea."

"Really? I thought wearing unshreddable clothes might be seen as politically incorrect for weres or something."

"Maybe that was true at some point, but not today." Knox shakes his head. "Things were different before every cell phone became a video camera. I've already gone viral with footage of my naked butt. You never know where people are hiding."

"Viral? You're joking."

"Have you seen the Central Park Ass Man meme? It's the one with a young naked guy who's walking away from the camera."

"That's you?" I pop my hand over my mouth. Come to think of it, that ass man had a certain swagger that is really familiar. "Oh yeah. That's you."

"Sign me up for sweats and a T-shirt. I'm in."

The two-tone doorbell sounds through the apartment, signaling that Alec has arrived with his lox and cream cheese. My inner wolf can smell them both from here.

"Food," she cries. *"Go, go, go!"*

I smile. It seems like my wolf has now fully recovered from the fight with Knox yesterday. I search into my soul, feeling the three kinds of magic swirl within me: witch, shifter, and fae. Today, I'll test out the lessons from my time with Knox. I'll channel that power into my wolf and keep her under control. Sure, it may not work perfectly, but I have to start somewhere.

Today is as good a place as any to begin.

CHAPTER 7

*I*t's late morning by the time Elle and I are navigating the crowded sidewalks of Canal Street.

Fae shopping central.

Humans crowd the sidewalk, as do vendors with pushcarts who sell everything from fake watches to real hot dogs. The smell of cheap perfume and cigarette smoke fills the air, as does the chatter of many voices.

I shake my head. "I still can't get over it. I always thought of Canal Street as the best place to get knock-off handbags. I can't believe that you-know-who are here." It's risky to say the word *fairies* in public, especially around tourists. Humans will whip out their cell phones and just start taking random video. In fact, I'm pretty sure that's how the Central Park Ass Man meme got started.

"This is *the* place for bargain you-know-who shopping," says Elle. We talked about this over bagels. Canal Street is the hidden base of operations for Belle's Basement, a secret discount super-store for fairies.

Who knew?

My best friend Elle, evidently.

"So let me get this straight," I whisper. "You have to give a gift to get inside the store. And then, you have to pay again to shop?"

Elle shrugs. "It's run by the you-know-whosies. We're lucky there are any rules at all."

That's my Elle. She rolls with the punches. Today, my best friend is wearing fitted jeans, tall black boots, and a sparkly blue tank that reads *"Bippity Boppity You."* Her sunglasses are perched atop her long blonde hair.

Damn, she looks like a million bucks.

For my part, I'm wearing mismatched flip-flops, a Christmas sweater-dress, and new orange sweats from the bodega. My brown hair is held back in a clip, and I wear no makeup. I'm like the ugly friend to the cool girl in class.

A chill crawls up my neck. I pause.

Elle stops beside me. "What's wrong?"

"I feel like we're being watched."

"If you've got a tail, the worst thing to do is stop." Elle tugs me back into the flow of sidewalk traffic. "It's probably just some fae wards you're detecting. There's only one fae shop around here, but they love to screw with humans."

"It's not the fae I'm concerned about."

"No? What's got you worried?"

I lower my voice. "Humans. Becoming a meme."

As if on cue, a little girl points at me as she walks by. "The brown-haired girl. She's got magic. Can I take a picture? Can I?"

The mother slows, considering. I think the Christmas sweater-dress must throw her off because she hauls her daughter off in the opposite direction. Elle and I share a long look and grin. We don't need to say anything; I know we're both thinking the same thing.

This really is an atrocious dress.

"Did you see that?" I ask. "Ever since I fought Jules, I have so much power inside me. Even some humans can sense it."

"Come on." Elle waves her hand dismissively. "She saw the

Christmas sweater, that's all. When you're little, you think a unicorn sweatshirt is a magical gift."

I rub my neck as if the motion can wipe away the sense I had before. All Elle's talk about gifts reminds me what we're going to do. "So the you-know-who need a gift to get in. What kind of gift did you bring?"

"It's not a big deal." Elle says that far too quickly, though. Which can only mean one thing.

It is totally a big deal.

"Elle. It's me. What did you bring?"

"Nothing major. This is Belle's Basement. It's not like we're at Nyxa's Boudoir."

At those words, a shiver rolls over my shoulders. "Queen Nyxa? You mean the crazy you-know-who from my birthday party?" We played a game of riddles because that's just what a nutso fae like Nyxa likes to do for fun. It was close, but in the end, I won and she took off. All in all, I consider myself very lucky to have survived the encounter alive. "*That* Nyxa runs a store?"

"Sure, what do you think she does?"

"Float around on a cloud, crunching on the bones of her victims."

"That's a rather specific image."

"Nyxa is a rather frightening you-know-whatsie."

"Well, I don't know about bone-crunching, but Nyxa definitely runs a high-end boutique." Elle pauses before one of the small storefronts. It's one of those deals where they roll up a steel door in the morning and line the store frame with bags galore. Since it's late morning, all the steel doors are open, and the storefronts are lined with bags that seem nailed into the brickwork around the garage-style entrance. The smell of roasting hot dogs and human sweat fills the air.

Sometimes, I wish my werewolf sense of smell would take a vacation.

I gesture at the storefront. "Is this the place?"

"Yup." Elle grabs my wrist. "You remember the rules?"

"You talk. I stand around and hide behind my, ahem, energy." *As in fae energy.*

"Because?"

"Elle." I roll my eyes. "I was raised by my aunties." Who were incredibly evil fairies, not that I need to say that part out loud.

"Whatever you think you know about your aunties and their people, you're about to see a side of them you never imagined. This is shopping. It makes them a little crazy."

"That would be something." My aunties used to throw quite a few parties. That's how Nyxa ended up at my birthday. I've seen drunken fairies. Eventually, they start to play Pin the Tail on the Human or Let's Start a Snowstorm in the penthouse. Not pretty.

Elle pulls me off into the store. It's a snug space that's surprisingly empty. That never happens in New York, but then again. Fairies. Who knows what enchantments they've cast here?

Elle looks over her shoulder, ensuring no one is within hearing distance. "Give me the rules one last time."

"Fine." There's no arguing with a bossy Elle. "I need to stay tapped into my fae power."

"Why?"

"If these fairies think I'm a human, then they'll try to torture and kill me."

"And if they detect that you're were or witch?"

"Then they'll still see me as a threat, and they'll try to torture me and kill me, too." According to Elle, the fae do a lot of torturing and killing while shopping.

"Good." Elle drags me deeper into the store. It's a classic Canal Street setup, so the tiny entrance extends into long rectangular space that seems to go on forever. Even so, this particular store stretches on even longer than usual. Elle pulls me past handbags, luggage, and some really cute silk shirts. After what feels like forever, we reach the far wall, which is a cramped square of space lined with fake pashmina scarves.

Elle pauses before the wall of scarves. She becomes so still, I wonder if she's even breathing. The air turns heavy with the sense of power. Silver dust motes twinkle in the air. I've felt power coming from Elle. Hers is warm and inviting. This stuff is chilly and prickly. I've never sensed fae magic quite like this before.

Which means its fae magic from a stranger.

My wolf perks up inside me. *"Danger is near. We should run."*

I roll my eyes. No matter what happens, my wolf's first reaction is to demand to run. *"Don't worry,"* I tell her in my soul. *"We're safe."* I try to tap into my different powers, but all the kinds of magic—fae, shifter, and witch—feel slippery in my mind. It's like trying to grab on to a liquid with your fist. Nothing stays put.

Disappointment wraps around me, heavy as a cloak. Most Magicorum spend their lives learning how to control their power. I've had weeks. Sometimes, it seems like an impossible task. Then, I picture my bare bum on YouTube.

Not happening. I'll keep working at it until I get it.

Elle raises her arm toward the wall of scarves. Screwing up her mouth, my bestie jams her hand into the layers of multicolored fabric. The sense of magic turns stronger. My wolf grumbles inside me.

"Our friend is hunting for something. This isn't safe."

"One more second." I work hard to keep up my super-calm inner voice. *"Be patient."*

Elle leans into the wall and gropes around for a bit. I'm about to ask if everything is okay when my bestie breaks out in an ear-to-ear grin.

"Got it," she whispers.

"Got what?"

Whipping her arm back, Elle yanks a small hairy creature

halfway out of the wall of scarves. The thing looks about two feet high and is made entirely of hair. "I've got It."

"It? That's a name." I tap my chin. "Wait? Didn't I see this guy in TV reruns from like a million years ago? *The Addams Family*, maybe?"

The little fae starts chattering away in some nonsense language. "It says that show was a knock-off. He is the original." More chattering. "And he says his name is Flaxengoober."

"Really?"

Elle shrugs. "I didn't name him."

I give the creature a half-wave. "Hey, Flaxengoober."

Elle keeps a handful of the creature's hair firmly grasped in her fist. "So, what's the price to get in, my friend?"

The thing chatters away in more nonsense-speak.

"That's fine, only I set the terms first."

More chattering. I make a mental note to ask Elle how she translates random fae languages so easily. Supposedly, there are thousands out there. Is the power of fairy translation something I can learn? Seems like it would come in handy.

"No," says Elle. "Terms first."

Flaxengoober yammers some more, but there's also a nodding motion from the pile of hair, so I figure that's a yes.

Elle smacks her lips. That's her thinking face, and making deals with the fae is very tricky. They can't lie, but they twist every word to their advantage.

"We want safe passage to go shopping." Elle looks to me. "And...I'm drawing a blank."

"We don't want to be tortured or killed while shopping."

"Right." Elle refocuses on Flaxengoober. "You heard her. And we want to be able to purchase something of our choosing for a fair price." She reaches into her jean pocket and pulls out a small locket. "And we'll pay with this."

It's a silver locket with a Hello Kitty emblem on it. Elle and I have worked this con before. I stifle a grin.

I set my hand on my throat. "You can't give that away. I know that locket. It's one of the few things you have from your mother." And by this I mean Elle's real mother, not the stepfamily of psychos who raised her.

Elle does have a locket from her mother, but it has a diamond-encrusted star on top of it, not a Hello Kitty. But these fae don't know about that. When working a con, it's always best to have a kernel of truth in there.

Sighing, Elle curls the locket against her chest. "I know. It means so much to me."

I lean in to the lie. "No, Elle. No, no, no." Maybe it's too much, but I'm starting to have a good time.

But like always, Elle's con works. The creature's hair comes to life, wraps around the locket, and sucks it into...whatever is going on under that pile of hair.

In the air, the silver dust motes sparkle to life again. They whirl into interlocking circles as the sense of magic intensifies. Elle releases her grip on Flaxengoober, who then disappears into the wall.

I grip Elle's hand. Her skin is clammy, just like mine.

We've done a lot of crazy things together. All of a sudden, I wonder if it's possible to push our schemes too far.

The wall of scarves opens down the center like the curtains being drawn on an old-time stage. Silver light pours in through the opening, casting everything in an odd glow.

Still hand in hand, Elle and I go inside. As we step into the brightness, I give myself another internal pep talk.

This is just another scheme, like all the others.

And this is me and Elle.

Together we're ready for anything.

CHAPTER 8

I may have been raised by fairies, but I still don't know much about the fae. Why? My so-called fairy aunties kept me locked in a penthouse with sketchy tutors. Plus, although Elle's a fairy, she's can't say much about the fae, either. It's all part of the magic that keeps her hidden from her evil stepfamily. Elle shares what she can, when she can, and I totally support that.

Long story short, I'm not sure what to expect when Elle and I walk through the wall that leads into Belle's Boutique. Turns out, we enter a small anteroom that's deserted, silent, and painted neon yellow. It reminds me of my aunties—they always wore bright colors. A small red door is painted with silver letters that read:

~~*Belle's Boutique*~~
 Now Under New Management
 Welcome to Ba Ba Bargains

Elle hisses in a breath. "Crap."

"Do you mean crap as in, 'Ba Ba Bargains will have much worse stuff than Belle's Boutique' or crap as in, 'we're in trouble?'"

"The second thing." Elle glances over her shoulder. "And the doorway back just disappeared." She nibbles on her thumbnail.

I narrow my eyes. Elle's always pretty calm. Thumb-nibbling only happens when we're about to get into serious trouble. In fact, the last time I saw this particular move, the Denarii headquarters was about to explode.

"You want to return to Canal Street?" I ask. "We just faked our way in here."

"Well, it's like this…" Elle winces. That's not a good sign. "You've heard how there are light and dark courts of fairies."

I nod. *This is one of the few things I do know.*

"Well, most fae don't hang at court; they live out in the wild. Or, at least they did before humans ruined nature and everything. That's why—"

"Stop right there." I raise my arms with my palms upright and facing Elle. "I can tell you're about to say something that'll make me worry."

Elle winces once more. "Yes."

"You know what?" I shrug. "Worrying won't help anything at this point. There's no doorway leading back, even if we wanted to go." I set my fists on my hips in what I hope is a confident pose. "We can do this."

Elle tilts her head. "So, you really don't want the details?"

"Is the plan the same? I tap into my fae energy so I seem like I'm one of them."

"Yup, and also keep your wolf from popping out."

"Definitely." I say this with confidence, but in all honesty? I have no idea how to use Knox's advice and keep my wolf inside me when she wants to come out and play. Oh, well. As Elle likes to say, *"No better time to learn than on a con."*

Unless, failing to learn means a bunch of angry fairies will curse you or kill you slowly. But there's not much I can do about it, so I put my trust in Elle.

Moving on.

"Then, let's go shopping." I straighten the neckline of my horrid Christmas sweater, grip the handle of the red door, and pull. As we step inside, I remind myself of my goals.

Successful shopping trip.

Unshreddable outfit.

No butt memes featuring yours truly.

Once inside, Ba Ba Bargains turns out to be a long and tall space that's also painted neon yellow. Tons of little fairies flit through the air. There are hundreds of green pixies, blue sprites, and even more multicolored butterfly types. In fact, there are so many fae, they make a great cloud of activity by the ceiling. And on the ground?

What the hey?

I blink hard, not sure what I'm seeing.

But no matter how many times I look, they're still there.

Sheep.

The store floor is covered with sheep-shaped fae who have pastel-colored wool and tiny wings. All of them drag around small wooden carts piled high with stuff. Small signs sit atop the fabric, reading things like *"Boy's Armor," "Women's Wing Cream,"* and *"Smiting Accessories."*

All of a sudden, I get why Elle wanted to warn me.

My wolf.

Instantly, my inner animal perks up. *"Sheep. Me want sheep."* She's both salivating and talking like Cookie Monster. That's a major red flag.

I try to tap into the power inside me, hoping to calm my wolf. Now, I don't have Alpha energy like Knox, but that's fine. I have tons of other magic to choose from. In my mind's eye, I picture the silvery threads of fae power that nest inside my soul. They're too slippery to get a good grip on, but I reach for them all the same.

Meanwhile, my inner wolf licks her chops and keeps right on talking like Cookie Monster. *"Me want sheep!"*

Not sure the inner power thing is working. I decide to go to my fallback position: logic.

"These are not sheep," I say. "They're fairies. Very powerful fairies."

"Like Colonel Mallory the Magnificent?" asks my wolf.

"Could be."

In all honesty, fairies with the power level of Colonel Mallory are extremely rare, so the chances are slim that one is bargain shopping at this very moment. Even so, I'm not telling my wolf that. She needs to stay calm.

"I don't like Colonel Mallory," grumbles my wolf. *"He placed that curse on me. Locked me up."* She's not happy, but she isn't trying to pop out of my skin, either. This is good.

All the while, Elle and I stand by the far wall. We haven't been noticed yet, and I'm figuring that's a good thing, considering we've got a good five feet on even the biggest fae here. Fairies will kill you for almost anything, and I have to imagine being larger than them is definitely on the list.

"How's your..." Elle makes a scratching motion with her hand.

"My wolf is okay."

"You sure? There's no door behind us, but there's still an exit. Let me know if you want to run for it." She gestures across the room to another small red door. Hard to miss.

I eye the door and consider my options. It's scary to stay here, but Elle and I have gotten this far, haven't we? I can't leave unless we at least try to get me some unshreddable stuff to wear.

"Nope, we're staying."

Elle exhales. "Good. Let's find you some clothes."

A sheep-fae lumbers past us, dragging along a green wooden cart with the words *"Mortal Repellent Spray"* written on the side in large orange letters. Up close, the sheep-fae looks so strange—human eyes in a pink wooly face—that a bubble of worry expands in my chest. "Wait a moment. You know how I said I didn't want information?"

"Uh-huh."

"Well, I changed my mind. What's with all the four legged—" My thoughts spin through what Elle said before about fairies and nature. My eyes widen as the truth appears. "Oh, wait. I've got it. The fae who created this shop, they used to live in the country-side, just like you were saying."

Elle nods. "Right."

"And where they used to live, there were lots of sheep."

"Right again. Over the years, they started to look like their surroundings, if you know what I mean. Humans got rid of their grazing lands back in the 1960's, so these fae came to live in New York."

I bob my head from side to side, thinking. "Okay. This isn't so weird really. The fae came to the city and got into retail. A lot of immigrants do that. What's there to worry about?"

Without waiting for Elle to comment, I take a cautious step toward another sheep-fae. This one's dragging a cart that reads *"Closeout Sale."* Sounds promising. Like all the rest of the sheep-fae, this one wears a little tiara with her name on it. Balinda.

I straighten my back and move closer. My wolf's not happy about it, but she spent years locked under a fairy spell, so my inner animal is doing her best to stay calm.

I can do this.

One step.

Two.

I'm almost to the cart when Balinda huffs, flaps her ridiculously tiny wings, and steps away. The scent of magic and mutton hits my nostrils.

My wolf—who has been keeping pretty sane up until now—starts to lose her mind.

"Sheep!" she screams inside my soul. *"Me want sheep!"*

"Look," I reply in my head. *"You need to stay calm."*

"SHEEP!"

Without meaning to, a low growl of frustration escapes my lips. And it's most definitely not human. A few yards away, Balinda pauses.

"How did you get in here?" asks Balinda. Needless to say, it's crazy-strange to have a pink sheep with human eyes start talking to you. "You're not fae."

I pull on my fairy power with everything I have inside me. It feels more slippery than ever. "I sure am fae."

In a smooth motion, Elle moves to stand between me and Balinda. "Hello, I'm Elle, and I am definitely fae." She grins and works her irresistible charm, complimenting Balinda's pretty wool and her tiara. Balinda smiles, sighs, and walks away, her little cart creaking behind her as she goes.

Elle turns to me. "How are we doing?" She makes that scratchy motion again.

"We've got time," I reply. "Just not a lot of it."

Inside, my wolf growls and snaps at the air. *"Me want sheep."*

"I got that," I say in my head. *"But you also don't want to be stuck under a spell again, right?"* This is a little mean of me, considering my wolf's past, but I'm getting desperate.

"Grrrr." My wolf isn't screaming to eat sheep, so I figure I have another minute or two at best.

Elle goes up on tiptoe and scans the store. "Bingo." She points at red exit door. "See what I see?"

By the door, there's a sheep with a cart marked *"Indestructible Muumuus."* Now a muumuu isn't my favorite kind of outfit, but at this point I'll take anything.

I give Elle a thumbs-up. "Let's do this."

Together, my best friend and I cautiously cross the sales floor. We're the only bipedal shoppers working the floor. The rest of the fae are still clustered around the ceiling. Thankfully, they're too concerned with fighting each other over good bargains to notice me and Elle. Even so, it would only take one wrong move and we'd have a thousand angry fairies after us. My throat constricts with worry.

Calm down, Bry. You and Elle have made it through sketchy places before. The key is to look harmless. Elle and I keep up our lazy pace.

Nothing to see here, just a few human-size fae out for a stroll. La-di-dah.

It seems to take forever, but eventually Elle and I make it halfway across the floor. Along the way, I get a pixie stuck in my hair, but I'm able to shake it off easily enough. The drone of fae above our heads turns deafening. It seems that there's a sale on fairy dust enhancer spray, whatever that is. High-pitched voices echo in my ears. It's like being trapped in a roomful of angry people inhaling helium.

"Grab it."

"That's mine."

"Back off."

At last, we make it across the room to the cart with indestructible muumuus. I step closer. The tiara on this sheep reads *"Barnicus."*

"Hello, uh. Barnicus."

Barnicus looks me over. Again, those human eyes in a sheep's face are downright weird. He doesn't reply.

This is working. Barnicus isn't running. I eye the cart greedily. It's shopping time.

With cautious steps, I move closer and reach toward the pile of neon-colored muumuus in the back of Barnicus's wagon. My hand is inches away from a bright yellow number when Barnicus stiffens. He looks over his shoulder at me and inhales. Deeply.

Oh, no. I forgot to keep trying to tap into my fairy power. My werewolf side must have leaked out. Who knew this multi-power stuff was so tricky?

Barnicus shivers so violently, his little wings shake. "Wolf," he whispers. "You're a wolf." This time, the sheep doesn't just lope away, he runs off like a shot.

This is bad. Prey should never run from a predator.

"SHEEPSHEEPSHEEP!" My wolf is clawing inside me. Fur ripples under my skin. I'm about to shift in a room full of sheep-fae. How exactly do I get myself into these situations again?

Elle saunters to my side and wraps her arm around my shoulder. "Bry, are you okay?"

All the blood in my body seems to drop to my toes. My bones start to snap and twist. Bolts of panic shoot through my nervous system.

"You can do this," says Elle in a soft voice. "You're fae. Remember that."

That's right. I'm part fairy, too.

Closing my eyes, I try to tap into my fae power. It stays slippery as ever. Frustration tightens down my limbs. Without meaning to, I let out another growl. This one is incredibly loud.

This time, the entire room falls silent. All eyes focus on me and Elle. Hundreds of fairies raise their arms. The sparkle of silver dust fills the air by their hands. Magic. The patrons here are going to cast a spell.

Barnicus shivers a short distance away. "I scented her," he cries. "Wolf."

In response, the fairy shoppers go berserk.

"Kill the beast!"

"Flay it!"

A bipedal sheep steps out onto the sales floor. She has baby-blue wool and a look that could freeze magma. Must be the store manager. This is getting worse by the second.

"On my mark," says the manager. "Pound her into the ground." She raises her fist, and the hundreds of fae lower their arms. The silver dust that was spinning about their arms breaks loose, taking the form of a massive arrow.

After that, it comes barreling right for me and Elle.

My bestie and I share a quick look before shouting the same word at the same time.

"Crap!"

Turning around, Elle and I make for the small red exit. We just get through and slam it shut behind us when the magic smashes into the closed door.

I exhale. *That was close.*

Elle and I have emerged into a snug alley. Some yards away, the foot traffic of Canal Street marches by.

Elle leans against the building's outer brick wall. "That was close."

I shake my head. "Didn't they promise not to hurt us?"

Elle rolls her eyes. "The sheep-fae who run the store didn't attack us. It was the customers. They made no such vow."

The hair on my neck stands on end. Once again, I have the horrible sensation of being watched. And in a Christmas sweater dress no less. From the corner of my eye, I catch a glimmer from Canal Street. It looks surprisingly like a camera.

Anger tightens through my limbs. I've had it with being followed. Whoever this is, I want to face them, once and for all.

"I'm going to catch them this time," I call to Elle.

"Catch who?"

"My stalkers. Watch this."

The shine of the camera came from where the alley meets the street. I rush off in that direction, stopping when I reach the sidewalk. I grip the brick wall so hard, I'm pretty sure I chip a few nails.

Humans stream by, but none seem to notice me. And certainly no one has a camera. I shake my head. All this stress is making me lose it.

Elle steps up behind me. "You know what? Your wolf actually did pretty well. You didn't shift or anything."

Lately, my insides always seem coiled with worry. At Elle's

words, some of that anxiety loosens. "That's true. I couldn't grab on to my fae power, but it was definitely an improvement."

"Besides, who wants to wear a muumuu?"

I stick out my tongue. "It was neon yellow, too."

Elle leans against the alley wall opposite mine. "So, what do you want to do?"

Now, I know my friend well enough to know what she's saying. *Do I want to keep going or give up?* Elle wouldn't judge me if I wanted to call it a day. I stare into the flow of humans along the sidewalk. Something deep inside my soul snaps. I'm done running away or hiding. What I want is something to wear as my badass werewolf self, so that's what I'm going to do. Maybe I should be all *who cares if people see me naked*, but guess what? I do care. And I'm going to do something about it. *For me.*

Only question left is: what do I want to do?

Folding my arms over my chest, I consider my options. In the end, there really is only one thing I can do. It's not pleasant, but I'm not giving up now.

"I'm not done shopping." I shoot Elle a sly grin. "Can you guess where we're going next?"

Elle meets my grin with one of her own. "Nyxa's Boudoir."

"Right on. Who cares if she's crazy? All the fae are nuts. At least, Nyxa's not a sheep."

Elle rushes out to the curb and yells a single word. "Taxi!"

Soon, my best friend and I are sliding into a yellow cab.

"Excelsior Club," says Elle.

As we tool across Manhattan, I check in on my wolf. Now that we're away from delicious-smelling sheep, she's calmer now. Although considering how we're going to Nyxa's Boudoir? Maybe things are about to get wild once more.

CHAPTER 9

*O*ur cab pulls up to a towering building on East 44th Street. The façade is all gray marble, bay windows, and inset metal crests. A bronze front stands dead center of the first floor. A tall doorman stands under the small red awning. A sign by the door reads *"Excelsior Club. Members Only."*

I lean until my nose presses against the cab's window glass. "Is this the place? It's mighty fancy."

"Wait until you see inside," says Elle. "Nyxa spares no expense on her boudoir."

My wolf perks up inside me. *"Will there be more sheep?"*

"Nope, not a single one," I reply in my mind. In all truth, I have no idea if any of those sheep-fae would hang out with Nyxa. That said, my wolf is salivating at just the mention of sheep. I'm not going to encourage this line of thinking.

I scooch over on the cab seat, push open the door, and step out onto the wide sidewalk. Elle marches past me, stopping when she's toe to toe with the doorman.

"We're here for Nyxa's Boudoir," announces Elle.

Inside my soul, I try grasping on to my fae powers. Like

always, they slip past my hold. Oh, well. Hopefully I'm working enough of a fairy vibe to fake my way into this store.

In reply, the doorman shakes his head from side to side. The motion is incredibly stiff, even for this part of town. He doesn't talk either, which is borderline rude.

Elle leans over so she talks right into the space between the doorman's pecs. "Hey, I'm fae. Let us in to Nyxa's already."

With more stiff movements, the doorman opens the chest-level buttons on his coat. Under the fabric, there's what looks like a tree trunk. A face is magically carved into the bark.

And then, the face speaks.

"It depends," says the doorman.

My mouth falls opens. This guy is a fairy who's made of wood. I didn't see that coming. No wonder his head movements were so stiff. That's not a head.

Inside my soul, my wolf takes an interest again. *"Is that a chew toy?"* she asks. Evidently, she now thinks all fae may be some kind of treat for her.

"Definitely not. Stay out of the way until we're away from the fairies."

"Why?"

"Colonel Mallory, remember?"

"Grr." That means my wolf remembers; she just doesn't want to talk about the fae who cursed her. Can't blame her for that. At least, my inner animal seems calm enough. For now, anyway.

Meanwhile, Elle straightens and pretends to find her manicure fascinating. "Depends on what?"

"What can you pay to get in?" asks the doorman.

Some tension loosens from my shoulders. We went through this before with the hairy guardian outside Ba Ba Bargains. Last time, Elle pawned a Hello Kitty locket on the guy. I can't wait to see what she comes up with next.

Elle raises her pointer finger. "First, I set the terms."

The doorman's wooden head—which is just for show—keeps watching the street. "Go on."

"We want safe passage to the store," says Elle. "And that means we don't want to be tortured or killed while shopping."

"Or afterwards," I add.

"Oh, that's good." Elle gives me a thumbs-up before facing the doorman again. "You heard her. Plus, we want to be able to purchase something of our choosing for a fair price."

"No tricks," says the doorman. "If you want in, I need something truly valuable." The way he says *truly valuable*, it's clear what he wants. Not something that costs money. More something that hurts Elle to the core to give up. The fae really are a twisted bunch.

"Not a problem." Elle reaches into her jean pocket and pulls out a small locket. "We'll pay for our entry with this."

My eyes widen. This is no Hello Kitty locket. This time, it's the real item. It's a platinum circle that's inset with a diamond star.

I try to shove Elle's arm down. "You can't give that away."

Elle turns, grips my shoulders, and meets my gaze straight on. I've seen this combination before--shoulder grips plus a steady stare means that Elle is about to say something she won't ever back down from.

"I know you, Bry. If you're not comfortable, you won't stay at West Lake. This keeps us together. It's important." She hands over the locket before I can stop her. With wooden movements, the doorman slips it into his pocket.

My hand touches to my throat. I know Elle is my best friend, but I've never felt our bond more than I have in this moment.

That said, there is no way I'm letting her give up the last thing she has from her birth mother.

"Get it back," growls my wolf inside me.

"On it."

As we walk into the store, I bump into the doorman. The big

wooden guy totters a little bit, and that's just the chance I need. As I pretend to right him again, I lift the locket from his jacket. I chuck his chin—which means rubbing my knuckles on the spot below his pecs—and head inside the Excelsior Club. It's very important when you're picking someone's pocket to make sure their touch focus is somewhere else.

I grip the locket more tightly and fight the urge to cheer. *I did it!*

Following Elle inside, I find the front door opens onto a little waiting room. It reminds me of the room before we got into Ba Ba Bargains, only this one is elaborate with its carved walls, velvet tapestries, and checkerboard marble floor. There's a large golden door on the other side of the room with elaborate loopy writing on it.

"Nyxa's Boudoir."

Elle sighs and stares at the lettering. "At least they aren't under new management." She seems so deflated and not-Elle, I can't wait to tell her the good news.

Gripping Elle's hand, I set the locket back onto her palm. "I believe this belongs to you."

She beams. "Bry, you're the best!"

"What can I say? I've picked up a few things over the years of hanging out with you."

"Picking the doorman's pocket." Elle sets the locket around her neck, making sure the diamond-encrusted locket is under her T-shirt. "Dang, I wish I'd thought of that."

"So far, it's Team Bry-Elle: 1, Team Nyxa: 0." I grip the golden handle. "How about we go rack up some more points?"

"Let's."

I yank open the door. A billow of smoke rolls out onto the

marble floor. Elle and I step inside a darkened room. *Nyxa's Boudoir.* The place is a lot of silver velvet curtains and wooden furniture painted in various shades of platinum. A dozen fairies lounge around on oversized pillows. At least they are all human-ish in shape, even if they are in shades of red, yellow, and green. Small tables dot the carpeted floor, all of them overflowing with different-colored ladies' undies.

"No sheep," says my wolf inside my soul.

"That's right," I confirm.

One tall pink fairy saunters toward us. She wears a snug evening gown that's cut to highlight her slim figure and long silver wings. "Welcome to Nyxa's. I'm Blythe. How may I help you?"

All of a sudden, my Christmas sweater outfit and frizzed-out hair seem especially awful. Blythe is so beautiful it almost hurts to look at her. My mouth starts moving on its own. "I'm looking for an enchanted outfit that won't shred if you change into a werewolf. Not for me. For a friend."

"It's a gift," adds Elle.

"I see," says Blythe. A glimmer of silver light encircles her raised right arm. Magic. Blythe's fae power shines brightly for a moment and then disappears. A pile of fabric now covers her arm. "You mean like this?" She lifts a series of clothing. "We have black leather pants, some black knee-high boots, and a cropped tank. Oh, there's also a long black duster coat. It's all self clean-ing, once every twenty-four hours."

My heart leaps into my throat. "Yes, that's perfect. What's the price?"

Blythe narrows her silver-green eyes. "A finger."

"How about this?" Elle raises her middle finger. "We pay you in fairy dust."

"Really?" Blythe's perfect eyebrows flicker upward. With magic disappearing from the world, fairy dust is at a premium. Blythe taps her lips with her long pink fingers. "How much?"

"Enough to fill a human tablespoon."

I happen to know Elle can sneeze and make that much fairy dust. She really is powerful. Before, Elle didn't tell me anything about her powers for fear her evil stepfamily would find her. Now, she's sharing more and more. I still worry every time she says anything. It's like her evil family will burst through the window at any second. Even so, Elle says it's her choice and I respect that.

"A human teaspoon," says Blythe breathlessly. "Agreed."

I bob on the balls of my feet. At this point, I could cheer, I'm so happy.

Blythe is about to hand over the pile of clothes when a column of silver dust appears in the center of the room. More magic. A sliver of unease worms its way through my soul.

Inside me, my wolf goes right on alert. *"Danger is coming,"* she growls.

"Agreed."

The silver fairy dust disappears. In its place, there stands Queen Nyxa. She looks as she did the last time I saw her: seven feet tall with orange skin and moss-green hair. Her crown, eyes, and floor-length gown are all pale blue. She looks at me and gasps. "You."

I give her a little wave. "Me."

Nyxa lifts her chin. "Are you here to request your boon?"

Now, the true answer goes something like this: *I am not crazy enough to chase you down for anything, let alone a boon. Because you are a sadistic nutjob who will twist the whole thing around and find some way to kill me.* But I do value my life, so I say something else instead.

"You owe me a boon?" I ask sweetly. I must do a good job of acting all innocent, because Elle shoots me a wink.

"You're here to force me into giving my boon."

I pinch the bridge of my nose. This is precisely why I didn't approach Nyxa to ask for my boon in the first place. I knew that

she'd do something just like this—say I'm forcing her into something—and then turn on the pain.

I force a smile. "No, the only reason I'm here is that I want to
buy this outfit. It's my—"

Nyxa snaps her fingers. Silver fairy dust encircles both me
and Elle. Fresh magic. I turn toward my friend, grasping through
the heavy silver haze. "Elle, are you—"

Before I can finish my sentence, the magical haze disappears.
A silver rope now encircles my head, the cord tied tightly
between my lips, I can barely breathe, let alone speak. The only
sounds I make are muffled grumbles. Elle lies curled by my feet,
trapped in an enchanted sleep.

My wolf loses her mind. *"We're trapped by fairies! Run!"*

"Stay calm," I coach her. *"The fae only hurt you worse if you run.
We should know; we're predators, too."* My animal stills inside my
soul, but I can tell it's the kind of shivering quiet that she usually
reserves for thunderstorms.

Nyxa walks a slow circle around me. "Do you want your boon?
Such a shame you need to say the words through that awful muzzle."

I scan the room. A dozen fairies and Nyxa. I've had some
battle training, but never against more than one or two oppo-
nents at a time. Nyxa grips my chin, forcing me to look at her.
She lifts her hand. Fresh fairy dust hovers above her palm. Nyxa
blows it in my direction. "Boo."

I check my limbs for fresh ropes, but there's nothing different
in my bindings. That's strange. It doesn't seem like Nyxa to send
magic in my direction without meaning to do harm. Before I can
think things through a little more, Nyxa starts speaking again.

"Your aunties were right about you," she says through a sneer.
"Too weak to fight."

Now, Nyxa may not know it, but those are the perfect words
for me in this moment. Nothing makes me come out fighting
harder than when my rebel-reflex kicks in.

Tell me I can't fight?

Just watch.

I reach into my soul, calling out to my wolf. *"Let's shift and take down anyone we can."*

There is no reply. I check my soul, finding that my wolf has been knocked out with the same enchanted sleep as Elle. That's what Nyxa did with the latest round of fairy dust. Not helpful.

Nyxa grips my chin even more tightly. "I heard how you went wolf and killed poor Jules. He was rather clever for a zombie. Such a shame you wouldn't marry him like your aunties wanted." Her eyes flare with an evil blue light. "Maybe I'll ask them here to witness your death." She turns to the other fae. "What do you say?"

They do a golfer's clap from their comfy cushions.

"Wonderful idea, Your Majesty."

"Make her pay."

Suddenly, the door from the reception room bursts open. A pair of wolves leaps into the room. One is colored in shades of gold; the other has scraggly black fur.

Oh, no.

I recognize their scents instantly. This is Hollywood and Abe. And the way they pace around me and growl at Nyxa? It's clear that they're here to help me and Elle escape.

Nyxa turns to me. "Who is this?"

I try to talk through my gag, but that's not happening.

"Oh, that's right. You can't speak." Nyxa raises her arm. "Let's see what we're dealing with here." More fairy dust encircles the two wolves. When the magic disappears, there stand a very naked Abe and Hollywood. They both grab handfuls of ladies undies to cover their private parts.

"Who are you?" asks Nyxa.

"We're Knox's pack," says Hollywood. He tosses his head of perfectly coiffed blond locks. "He's our Alpha."

"Only, he hasn't accepted that yet," says Abe. "But we're trying to prove ourselves."

Hollywood rolls his eyes. "Abe, you don't have to be honest about everything."

Abe keeps right on talking. "Did Knox say anything about what happened at Lucky's? We were there to help protect you, Your Majesty. Was he impressed? You're clearly our queen, so we appointed ourselves knights in your court."

A sly smile rounds Nyxa's mouth. "Wolves have courts?"

"Oh, Hollywood made that part up." Abe grins. "He's going to be Knox's beta, and he's really smart." He turns to me lifts his chin. "So we're your knights."

Surprisingly enough, it's really cool to find out that you have knights, even if they made up the title themselves and tell you about it while naked and covering their junk with bras. It's the thought that counts, really.

Nyxa mock-sniffs. "This is...so touching. I'll keep it in mind as I flay you. I'll even keep you awake for the duration, so we can all enjoy your screams." The room of fae start up their golfer's claps again.

I may not be able to shift into my wolf form, but I do still know a thing or two about self-defense. And I know enough to realize that once the baddie starts talking about flaying, it's time for me to get my fight on.

Picking up a display table by one leg, I swing the entire thing right at Nyxa's face. It impacts into her cheek with a satisfying crack.

At the same time, Abe and Hollywood transform into their wolf forms and leap straight at Nyxa. The other fairies slowly rise from their lounge pillows. Evidently, fighting breaks out in Nyxa's Boudoir fairly often, because the dozen of them don't seem too shocked.

Working together, Wolf-Abe and Wolf-Hollywood have Nyxa

pinned to the ground. She's screaming and flailing around, but she isn't getting up. Yet.

The dozen other fae stand in a loose circle around us. Silver dust sparkles around their raised arms.

Kneeling beside Elle, I shake her shoulders. "Wake up! We don't have much time. We have to run."

While still holding Nyxa down, Wolf-Hollywood motions with his head toward the exit door. I know what he wants: me to leave.

There's no way I'm going anywhere without Elle.

The fairies around us release the fairy dust from around their arms. A haze of silver motes and magic comes flying at me, Elle, Wolf-Abe, and Wolf-Hollywood. The haze surrounds us for a moment. When it fades, I find myself kneeling beside Elle's sleeping form. My ankles and wrists are tied behind me. Abe and Hollywood are trussed up with ropes as well.

Nyxa slowly rises to stand. "Thank you, my sweetlings." She brushes her fingers over her chin. There's a cut along her jawline. Nyxa glares at me. "I'll kill you extra slowly for that."

Blythe steps forward. "My queen, the two girls have magical protection while they are in your store."

Nyxa rolls her eyes. "Then we'll transport them somewhere else, won't we?"

Blythe bows. "My queen, that would require a lot of fairy dust. You're already—"

"Enough!" Nyxa folds her arms over her chest. "We all know I have enough fairy power to last a hundred years. I could transport all of you anywhere."

In other words, Nyxa is low on fae power. Good to know.

Nyxa raises her hand. "No, I have a much better death in mind. We leave the girls here to die of starvation, right beside the dead carcasses of their friends. That's brilliant, isn't it?"

More golfer's claps erupt around the room. The fae really are evil.

"Let's get this started." Nyxa waves her arm. More fairy dust flies off her hand. This time, the magical haze encircles the room. Once it disappears, I can see that all the ornately carved walls are gone. Instead the place is nothing but bricks.

Oh, no. We're magically bricked in. No exit.

Nyxa stalks over to Wolf-Abe and Wolf-Hollywood. They are writhing under her bonds. Nyxa kicks at them with her slippered foot. "I can kill these then. They aren't under any protection." She glares at me. "And then, I'll have you dragged out into the alley to finish you there. Not because I don't have the power for a transport, but because it pleases me to have you die that way."

I pull at the bonds around my wrists and feet. The silver cords bite into my skin. They don't loosen in the slightest, though. My heart pounds so hard, I can feel its beat in my throat. That's when I remember it.

My cell phone.

I wiggle with all my strength, working my cell free from my back pocket. Closing my eyes, I try to picture the keyboard. What and where do I push to send a text to Knox? My emergency code is TBL. With all my focus, I dip into the power inside my soul. This time, I don't so much try to grip my fae power as direct it. Silver glimmers shine under my eyelids.

For the first time, fae power trickles through me. My cell phone beeps. In my mind, I can see the magic type in a message to Knox.

Pain explodes across my cheek, snapping me out of my reverie. Opening my eyes, I find that Nyxa now kneels before me. "How about we play?" Reaching out, she wraps her fingers around my throat and starts to squeeze. Every nerve ending in my body goes on alert. My shoulders heave with the attempt to pull in breath, but Nyxa is too strong. My mind becomes a riot of fear; it's impossible to tap into my powers again.

I struggle under Nyxa's grip, but it's no use. As the minutes pass, my movements become more sluggish while my thoughts turn more frenzied. A low thudding sounds in my head. At first, I think it's my heart, but I realize that's not what happening at all.

Someone is banging on brick walls. The faintest scent floats on the air.

Sandalwood and musk.

It's Knox. He must have gotten my emergency text and got here super-fast. I don't know what makes me more excited; the fact that my magic worked to help me text or that Knox is here so quickly.

Who am I kidding? I'm happier that Knox is here, definitely.

Nyxa releases my throat. I hunch over, gasping for breath. "Oh, my." She focuses her attention on Knox. "Another intruder to kill. It's turning into an interesting day. I shall make him turn boneless. That's always entertaining."

Knox? Boneless?

Never.

Power and rage erupt through my soul. Colored lights dance in my vision: golden for shifter, red for witch, and silver for fae. They all course through me, but the fae power is now the easiest for me to direct. Silver haze encircles my body. The bonds snap. I rise and lift my arms. A blast of silver energy pours off my palms and slams into the wall. The bricks shatter under the magical blast.

Knox stands on the other side of the new opening in the wall. His face is tight with rage. With a great roar, his wolf bursts free from him as he leaps into the room. Knox races over to Abe and Hollywood and bites through their cords. Now, Knox, Abe, and Hollywood encircle me in a protective ring.

I'm not the kind to stand around when there is work to do, especially now that I know how to focus my fae energy. It would be great to tap into the witch power as well, but heck, I just got a hold of the fairy stuff. There's no point being greedy. Closing my eyes, I pull on the well of fairy energy, imagining it enveloping my wolf. In my mind, I see my wolf surrounded in a silver haze. The glowing motes of power settle into her white fur.

My wolf awakens.

I focus the power again, commanding her to appear.

Fur appears on my limbs. Muscles reform. Teeth lengthen. My wolf form bursts free. The sense of freedom and power thrums through my veins. I take my place in my pack. With my mate. Moving on instinct, we all turn to face Nyxa.

Nyxa takes a half step backward. "I command you to leave my presence." But her words come out as a half whisper.

Nyxa is afraid.

As well she should be.

Knox and I share a quick look. There's no need to speak. We both know what we want to do. Leaning back on our haunches, we spring forward and attack. Tables go flying. I grab Nyxa by the arm and toss her against the wall. I nip another fae in the ankles, making him tumble over. Once the guy is prone, I jam my head under him and flip up. The fae slams into the ceiling with a *thwack*.

Wow. The fairies are really toss-friendly. No wonder they're terrified of wolves.

The wolf forms of Knox, Abe, and Hollywood go after other fae, too. Soon, it's not so much a fight as a game of catch. We move too quickly for them to summon up any fairy dust. Although, considering how rare the stuff is in the first place—and how much they wasted before Knox arrived—I wouldn't be surprised if they ran out anyway.

At some point, Nyxa comes to. For a second, I think she might rejoin the battle, but that's not in the cards. Instead, Nyxa races from the room. Once their queen retreats, the rest of her court follows along closely behind her.

Wolf-Knox looks to me. "Want us to kill them?"

Some of the fairy power I'd awakened now speaks to my soul. "No, there are too few Magicorum left."

Wolf-Knox sniffs. "Nyxa is a nightmare."

I shrug. "She's a fae who's being a fae."

Knox nuzzles into the fur on my neck. "You're too good."

"I don't know what I am, really." I shift my weight from foot to foot. "I only know that it feels wrong to destroy someone unless they are attacking."

Nearby, a swirl of red light appears on the torn-up carpet. Fresh magic, and since it's red, this power is of the wizard variety. The crimson light disappears. In its place stands Alec. He's wearing jeans, a blue blazer, and a grin. "What did I miss?"

"How did you know I was here?" asks Wolf-Knox.

"I slapped a tracking spell on you because, well, you're Knox. If there's something to kill, you'll get into a fight." Alec lets out a low whistle. "Looks like I missed a doozy." He scans the room, his gaze landing on Elle's sleeping form. "No!"

"She's fine," I say quickly. It's awkward to talk in my wolf form. The long canines always get in the way. "It's a sleeping enchantment."

Alec kneels beside Elle and pulls a large gemstone from his pocket. Holding the stone in his palm, he whispers an incantation. The gem lights up crimson, the seams of brightness shining through his fingers. Beams of red fall across Elle's sleeping face. A second later, she opens her eyes.

"What happened?" asks Elle.

"You and Bry got into another caper." Alec's tone is so gentle and sweet. "Are you all right?"

Elle sits up and rubs her neck. "Sleeping spells. Why does it always have to be sleeping spells?" She points at me. "That's your jam, not mine."

"Maybe we've been hanging out too long. My Sleeping Beauty life template might be rubbing off on you."

Wolf-Knox raises his paw. "Bry called me her king, too."

"Hey," I playfully nip at him. "I thought we agreed you were my not-so-charming prince. This is a coup."

Wolf-Knox mouths one word: *king.*

"Well, Your Highness." Alec stands and then gently assists Elle to her feet, too. "How many am I transporting?"

Wolf-Knox looks at Abe and Hollywood. "Definitely Elle and Bry," he says to Alec.

I nudge Wolf-Knox with my muzzle and stare pointedly across the room. Wolf-Abe and Wolf-Hollywood and droopy ears and tails. "Just me and Elle?" I ask.

Wolf-Knox pauses for a long moment before letting out a long sigh. "Transport Abe and Hollywood, too."

Wolf-Abe and Wolf-Hollywood start yipping with glee. "Don't get any ideas," warns Wolf-Knox. "We're not pack."

The yipping instantly stops. *Poor Abe and Hollywood.*

Wolf-Knox swings his massive head toward Alec. "Can you send these two...back to wherever's their home? You can do that, yeah?"

Alec flashes his most toothy grin. "For not-pack members, I do such things all the time." He fishes in his pocket and brings out more gems. "This ought to do it." Alec raises his voice and addresses the room. "Everyone, over here."

There is no way I'm switching to my human form now—there are way too many people around. So, I stay all wolfed up as I cross the torn-up shop floor.

That's when I spy it.

My unshreddable outfit.

Still sitting in a pile where Blythe dropped it.

Now it's my turn to yip with joy. "My clothes are still here. Can you grab them, Elle?"

"My pleasure." Elle steps over and scoops the items in her arms. "This stuff is the bomb." Once she has the items in hand, we all go to stand near Alec.

Alec rubs the gemstones between his palms. "Everyone ready to go?" He poses the question to the group, but for some reason, all eyes have focused on me. Not sure when I became leader of this party, but I like it.

"Yes," I answer. "Let's go home."

Alec casts the spell, and we all go home, including me with my new outfit. All in all, this makes of the best capers Elle and I have ever had.

And that's saying something.

I take another turn on the highway. Knox and I are riding his Harley up to Bear Mountain. The lowering sun paints the trees in shades of yellow and orange. Is there any better feeling than riding with your best guy pressed up behind you?

Hard to think of one at the moment.

Now that my wolf is under control, Knox has been teaching me to ride. His Harley is a little large for me, but I'm getting used to it. Knox leans against my back and wraps his arms more tightly around my waist.

My inner wolf pipes up. *"We do so love to ride."*

I have to agree with her.

Although I've gotten my shifting under control, I'm still not taking any chances with my wardrobe. Today, I'm wearing what's become my go-to outfit: my unshreddable black leather pants, duster, cropped tank, and boots. And they are self-cleaning, just like Blythe promised. When we went fae shopping a week ago, I never thought I'd get an outfit as awesome as this one.

Then again, I never thought I'd fight Nyxa and channel my fae powers, either.

How things change.

Shifting my weight, I make the turn onto the back roads that lead to Bear Mountain. I'm not supposed to know this, but we're going to Bear Mountain for a very specific reason. Knox is throwing me a surprise party. It's to replace the art opening that we never actually made it to. The goal was so I could get to know kids from West Lake Prep; Knox wanted to make sure I didn't miss out. He tried to hide it from me, really. But I guess it's one of these wolf-mate things. Hard to hide anything from each other.

Although I did add in a little surprise of my own. It will be interesting to see if he figures it out.

We pull up to our favorite spot to park—a knot of trees by a small toolshed—and I kill the engine. Now that the bike isn't roaring anymore, I barely make out the sounds of a drum and cymbal. There must be a band getting ready to set up.

"Did you hear that?" I ask, trying to look surprised. "Could that be a rock band getting set up?"

Knox nips my ear. "Might be." My mate isn't getting off the bike. Plus, he's still got his arms wrapped about my middle.

"Sounds like it's about a quarter-mile away. Could this be a party?"

Knox chuckles, low and soft. "Not surprised at all, are you?"

"No, it's the bond between us."

"I'm never going to be able to keep birthday presents secret now."

"Hey, it wasn't a surprise, but I'm still so happy about it. You're a thoughtful mate."

Knox gives my waist a squeeze. "What was that word?"

"Thoughtful?"

"No, you know what one I mean." Even though we're obviously together, I've still been a little squeamish about using the word *mate* around Knox.

"Oh," I pause for dramatic effect. "Mate."

"That's the one." Knox hoists himself off the bike and then

scoops me into his arms. If I liked the sensation of riding a bike with Knox, I love the feel of being curled up against his chest. His ice-blue eyes lock with mine as he twirls us around. "Say it again."

My face turns about three shades of red. "Mate."

Knox leans in until our mouths are about touching. "That's the one." His lips brush against mine in the barest of touches. I'm hoping this will turn into a full-blown kiss when a familiar set of scents waft in from the woods around us.

Abe and Hollywood.

Knox sets me back on my feet. He's frowning, but there's no real anger in him. "Hey, now. I didn't invite them."

I flash my palms in a classic jazz hands move. "Surprise."

Knox gives me one of those deep chuckles that I love. "Well, I have to admit, I did not see this coming."

"They're just heading off to the party," I say. "They weren't going to interrupt us. We just happened to catch their scent."

Knox tilts his head. "How did you know that?"

Closing my eyes, I search my soul. How did I know that, exactly? I feel a pull on my rib cage—a thread of connection that reaches out from me and ends with Abe, Hollywood, and Knox.

Inside my soul, my wolf raises her voice. *"You know who they are,"* she says.

"I do," I reply.

I link my fingers with Knox's. His touch is warm and firm. "I know where Abe and Hollywood are going…because we're pack."

"Yeah," Knox sighs. "I can sense them, too."

"We don't have to do anything about it. I know how you feel about taking on hundreds of wolves."

"But it's not hundreds of wolves. It's Abe and Hollywood. You want them around?"

I purse my lips. Do I want more people dependent on me? What does it even mean to be the mate of a pack Alpha? As the questions hit my mind, my wolf starts chanting inside my mind.

"Pack! Pack! Pack!"

I shake my head. "My wolf certainly does."

Knox lowers his voice. "Yeah, and what about you?"

The answer tumbles form my lips, fully formed. And the moment I speak the words, I know that they're true. "I do want them around. I'm a Bryar Rose life template. That means I'm supposed to be a princess with a court."

"They told you about the knights thing?" Knox tries to look serious, but there's no hiding the smile that rounds his lips. "Those guys."

"Why shouldn't I have a court? I've already found my, you know..."

Knox grins. "Are you saying I'm your prince?"

I hold my thumb and forefinger slightly apart. "A little."

"Good, because it's true. I'm a prince of a guy. Incredibly charming."

"More like moody."

"And handsome."

I roll my eyes. "Not to mention humble."

Knox cups my face in his hands. "And lucky."

My face reddens. Whenever Knox gets sweet, I can't help but blush. "We're both lucky."

"I've got an idea. Why don't we give Abe and Hollywood the good news?" He slides his arms around my waist and twirls me around again. "And then we can dance. You may not know this, but dancing is one of my most princely qualities."

"I never should have said that prince thing. I'll never live it down."

"Let's find the music, Bryar Rose. Nothing more fun than dancing and kissing in the moonlight."

And so that's exactly what we do.

The End

The adventure continues in SHIFTERS AND GLYPHS,
Book 2 in the Fairy Tales of the Magicorum

ANGELBOUND BY CHRISTINA BAUER

The best selling paranormal romance series with more than a million copies sold

Follow the adventures of Myla Lewis, a quasi-demon girl who's the most powerful gladiator-style warrior in Purgatory. Myla kicks ass across the after-realms—aka the supernatural lands of ghouls, demons, angels, and demon-fighting thrax—as she destroys evil, falls in love, and discovers her true role in a mysterious prophecy.

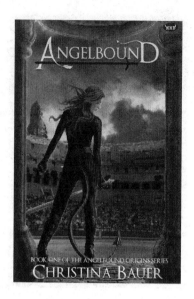

SCYTHE BY CHRISTINA BAUER

"Fans of A Wrinkle in Time can't miss **Dimension Drift***!" - Christina Trevaskis,* **The Book Matchmaker**

Don't miss the first prequel novella in the new science fiction series from best selling author Christina Bauer!

Follow the adventures of Meimi Archer, a science genius who attends aLearning Squirrel High, a "school" with a lot of useless lesson plans and one brooding hottie.

Things go downhill from there.

MAGICORUM BY CHRISTINA BAUER

A modern fairy tale series that **USA Today** *calls "Must Read YA Paranormal Romance"*

Enter a world that's a lot like our own...only fairies, shifters, and wizards are REAL. They're called the Magicorum, only their supernatural power is disappearing. This series will lead you through the lives of three of them, starting with Bryar Rose (Sleeping Beauty).

BEHOLDER BY CHRISTINA BAUER

The epic fantasy series that's been compared to **Game of Thrones**

Follow the adventures of Elea, a simple farm girl who must tap into her witchy powers in order to defeat an evil Tsar. Join Elea as she learns the magick of skeleton and spirit… All while falling for a mysterious mage named Rowan.

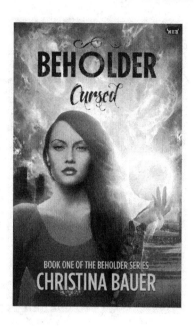

IF YOU ENJOYED THIS BOOK...

...Please consider leaving a review, even if it's just a line or two. Every bit truly helps, especially for those of us who don't *write by the numbers,* if you know what I mean. Plus I have it on good authority that every time you review an indie author, somewhere an angel gets a mocha latte. For reals.

And angels need their caffeine, too.

ACKNOWLEDGMENTS

Gulp.

Double gulp.

I'm taking the plunge and have decided to become an author full time.

Yipes!

Did I mention that I'm freaking out? Well, I am.

Here's the story on my full time fears. On the next few pages, you'll see the somewhat insane list of books that have been lurking in my brain and can now get OUT OF MY FREAKING HEAD over the next few years. I'm told it's too aggressive and might overwhelm you, my dear readership.

Eep.

Still, I can't help it. Stories churn around my soul. If don't release them in time, I worry they'll evaporate into the ethos. Besides, my internal reality is really fractured. It helps to share it with others who go: *wow, that's kind of cool!*

So there you have it. Thanks in advance for your support and understanding, because I'll definitely do something stupid as I make this journey. But no matter what turns this path may take,

I'd like to commence by showing my appreciation to the team of crazies who've helped make this all possible.

First, there is the amazing team at Inscribe Digital. They believed in me and my vision from the start. Thank you, Kelly Peterson, Ana Szaky, Katy Beehler, and Allison Davis. You're marvels!!!

Next, there's the wonderful team at Monster House Books. Arely Zimmermann, where would I be without you? I shiver to even think about. Plus, I'm incredibly proud to see you grow as a businesswoman and editor.

And I can never forget you, my dear readers and bloggers. You guys are the best, end of story. Thank you for every high five, sweet idea, and suggested change. Mwah!

Most importantly, my deepest appreciation goes out to my husband and son. Your patience and support mean everything. I love you both with all my heart and soul.

COLLECTED WORKS

Angelbound Origins

About a quasi (part demon and part human) girl who loves kicking butt in Purgatory's Arena

.5 Duty Bound – a prequel from Prince Lincoln

1. Angelbound

1.5 Lincoln – the events of Angelbound as told by Prince Lincoln

2. Scala

3. Acca

4. Thrax

5. The Dark Lands

6. The Brutal Time (Fall 2019)

7. Armageddon (already here, long story!)

Angelbound Offspring

The next generation takes on Heaven, Hell, and everything in between

1. Maxon

2. Portia

3. Zinnia (Summer 2019)

4. Kaps (Summer 2020)

5. Huntress (Summer 2021)

Angelbound Worlds

Inside stories about your fav characters

1. Xavier (Spring 2020)

2. Cissy (Spring 2021)

Beholder

Where a medieval farm girl discovers necromancy and true love

1. Cursed

2. Concealed

3. Cherished

4. Crowned

5. Cradled

Fairy Tales of the Magicorum

Modern fairy tales with sass, action, and romance

1. Wolves and Roses

1.5 Moonlight and Midtown

2. Shifters and Glyphs

3. Slippers and Thieves (Fall 2019)

4. Bandits and Ballgowns (Fall 2020)

Dimension Drift

Dystopian adventures with science, snark, and hot aliens

Prequels

1. Scythe

2. Umbra

Novels

1. Alien Minds (Spring 2019)

2. ECHO Academy (Spring 2020)

3. Drift Warrior (Spring 2021)

Publisher's Note: Christina Bauer is a non-linear thinker who came up with ARMAGEDDON and then went back and wrote some earlier books. This is why you'll see ARMAGEDDON (Book 7) and the Offspring series available before THE BRUTAL TIME (Book 6). We've told her to stop this practice, but she keeps giving us lewd hand gestures in response. Apologies in advance for any inconvenience.

ABOUT CHRISTINA BAUER

Christina Bauer thinks that fantasy books are like bacon: they just make life better. All of which is why she writes romance novels that feature demons, dragons, wizards, witches, elves, elementals, and a bunch of random stuff that she brainstorms while riding the Boston T. Oh, and she includes lots of humor and kick-ass chicks, too. Christina lives in Newton, MA with her husband, son, and semi-insane golden retriever, Ruby.

Stalk Christina on Social Media – She Loves It!
    Blog:
http://monsterhousebooks.com/blog/category/christina
    Facebook: https://www.facebook.com/authorBauer/
    Twitter: @CB_Bauer
    Instagram: https://www.instagram.com/christina_cb_bauer/
    Web site: www.bauersbooks.com

SUBSCRIBE

Get a FREE copy of Christina Bauer's novella, BEVERLY HILLS VAMPIRE, when you sign up for her personal newsletter: https://tinyurl.com/bauersbooks
   Not available in stores

A NOVELLA BY
CHRISTINA BAUER